KING OF CHAOS

Mat Waugh

www.matwaugh.co.uk

Produced by Big Red Button Books, a division of Say So Media Ltd.

ISBN: 978-1-9763-8962-7

Published: October 2017

MAT WAUGH

KING OF CHAOS

BOOK 3

For Anne and Peter,
and a childhood built with words.

And for Kate, always.
(But if the kids wake tonight, it's your turn.)

Contents

Very Important Message

**If your Mum, Dad or Auntie don't get emails
from Mat Waugh, they don't love you enough.**

*There, I've said it. Instead all they'll receive are
emails like* Re: application to put your child in
prison *and* 50 Meals Made from Cabbage. *But it
also means they won't know about my new Charlie
stories. And most importantly, you can't GET MY
FREE CHARLIE BOOK!*

*Get them signed up. There's info at the back of this
book and I'll pretend I didn't write this bit.*

*What? They are already signed up? Hey, that means
they do love you after all! Happy reading!*

Harry

Charlie Fact File

This is Book Three about my crazy little brother Charlie. But don't worry if you haven't read the other two books yet because it really doesn't matter. Read them afterwards. Or backwards.

Here are the only ten things you need to know.

1. My name is Harry. I'm eight. I'm a girl. Yes, I know it's a funny name for a girl. You'll need to get over it.

2. My brother is three. He's called Charlie, but any aliens listening to my Mum will think his name is *Oh Dear.* Can you guess why?

3. Charlie found five Rice Krispies in his tummy button last night. We ran out of Rice Krispies a month a go.

4. My Dad isn't nearly as funny as he thinks he is. But he is still quite funny.

5. I have a Granny who's quite strict. She broke her leg on a car, and now Dad says she'll never be able to play professional rugby again. It's very sad.

6. Charlie wears nappy pants. He's too old for nappy pants. But you have to admit that they are a useful place to store your snacks if you don't have pockets.

7. Charlie is rubbish at speaking. Right now it's cute, but if he does it when he's 24 everyone will laugh at him and probably put him in a zoo. Mum must be worried.

8. We go on lots of trips to places. I think Mum and Dad are easily bored. But then they take us to boring places. It's weird.

9. My friends at school think Charlie is great. My best friend Aileen says she'd like to borrow him for the holiday, like a stick insect. I'm going to ask my Mum.

10. Charlie loves chocolate. I love chocolate. Charlie loves TV. I love TV. Charlie loves sitting on my lap. I love Charlie sitting on my lap. Charlie loves trumping on me. I'm not so keen on that.

Right, now you know everything. Let's begin!

Mirror Mirror

I've got an idea. Let's compare our list of The World's Most Boring Shops. You know, the ones that make you want to yawn before you've even got out of the car.

What about supermarkets? I've tricked you there, because if you put that on your list, sorry but I think you're wrong. They're not all good, of course. Mum always gets me to fetch the washing powder, and it weighs about the same as Charlie. She says I'm too slow to do the self checkout myself. And she always buys too many vegetables. But what about the trolleys? Or sweets? What about trying to sneak your favourite snacks into the trolley? I bet you didn't think of all that. So no, supermarkets shouldn't be on the list.

Garden centres? Yes, I'll let you have that one

if you said it. We don't go there much, not since Charlie found a stepladder next to the packets of seeds. He pulled armfuls of them off the racks and scattered the brightly coloured packets on the floor – sunflowers, daisies, nasturtiums, cornflowers, marigolds, lupins and more.

'Charlie!' Mum had shouted, running over from the *Reduced for Quick Sale* section. 'Have you gone mad?'

'I not mad,' said Charlie sadly, sitting in the middle of the pile of seeds. 'I just want to play pairs wiv someone.' He turned over a Sunflower and a Marigold, and turned to face Mum.

'Bum-bum. No pair. Your turn?'

What about a wine shop? Now that's *really* boring. They only sell five things: red, white, pink, fizzy and beer. You'd think we'd only be in there for five minutes. But Dad take two hours to choose, holding Charlie by the hood in case he breaks anything, and then he just gets the one on offer anyway.

But here's one I bet you didn't say – the tile shop. Do you remember when we had all that building work done, and Charlie did something very silly with Grandad's medals? That was in the first book, so you might not remember it. But about the same time Mum and Dad started dragging us around town, looking for stuff to put on the walls when the building work was finished. And that's how we ended up at Tile Town, otherwise known as The Shop Where Harry Nearly Died of Boredom.

There were grumpy notices everywhere.

Beware of Forklift Trucks!

Tile stacks are Dangerous!

No walking in Display bathrooms!

Children under Control at ALL TIMES!

They should just have put up a big sign on the front of the store saying **We're not very friendly and you should buy your tiles somewhere else.**

'Dis one?' said Charlie as we walked past the first pile of tiles – brown, with cream flowers on them. In front of each pile there was a little stand with number cards in it, so you could take one to the counter to order some.

'Those old fashioned ones?' smiled Dad. 'I'm

not quite ready to turn into your Granny.'

'Oi,' said Mum. 'That's my mother you're talking about. And her bathroom is very nice. Very… traditional.'

'Dis one?' Charlie's new pick was big white tiles, with blue stripes. Charlie took a card and slipped it into his dungarees pocket.

'Looks like toothpaste,' I said.

'Not quite right,' said Mum.

'Dis one?'

'Not on your life,' said Dad.

'What about DIS one?' Charlie stood with his hands on his hips. We hadn't even got half way down the first aisle.

'Look, we need a bit of time to choose,' said Mum. 'Why don't you and Harry have a look around, see if you can find any ones you really like? Then Dad and I can have a browse in peace.' A skinny, grumpy lady in a shop uniform was staring at us from the end of the aisle. 'Just don't let Charlie go climbing on anything,' said Mum quietly.

So I took Charlie's hand and we trotted off, followed at a distance by the grump. Charlie waved at her, but she didn't wave back. 'She tired,

I fink,' he decided. 'Maybe she needs a nap.'

Every aisle was almost identical. Pile upon pile of white, brown or cream tiles; some square, some rectangular, some like stone, some like wood, but all of them boring. I put my arms out and pretended the lines on the floor were high wires, and I was balancing above Niagara Falls. Meanwhile Charlie took a card for any of the designs he liked.

'Dis one looks like snow... dis one looks like sticks... dis one looks like swimming pool... ' At one point, as he put his foot on a pallet to reach up for a card, there was a loud hissing noise. We looked up: the grump was baring her yellow, snaggly teeth at us, and waving a bony finger.

'Can't you read? Get down!' she rasped.

'No, I not read,' said Charlie matter-of-factly. 'I'm free.'

'Three,' I corrected, automatically.

'And you is a bit too crotchety, anyway.' Crotchety was Charlie's new favourite word. He turned his back on her, and we walked on.

In the back corner we found something a bit more interesting. Cubicles had been tiled to look like bathrooms; some of them even had toilets and sinks in them. They'd put the most interesting tiles here, too, if you can say tiles are interesting, which I don't think you can.

'Wow!' said Charlie. 'Is like a party!' He was standing in front of a bathroom that glittered and sparkled. Small mirrored tiles lined one wall, as if a disco ball had been rolled out flat. On the other wall was a rainbow of shimmering coloured squares: deep, sweet-wrapper purple, sparkling lipstick red, vivid broccoli green, eye-popping lemon yellow and more. All of these colours were reflected in the wall opposite, and the effect was magical.

'Wow,' said Charlie again, taking a handful of cards.

'Put those back.' The store witch had crept up behind us, and croaked her warning right over my shoulder with her stinky coffee breath. Charlie grabbed hold of my leg.

'We're just looking!' I said.

'Well you don't *look* with your grubby fingers, do you?' she said, like grown-ups do. And she reached out and grabbed the cards from Charlie's hand, and shoved them back into the display.

'You need a lie down!' said Charlie crossly. A new thought occurred to him, and he put his head on one side, looking up and down at her from behind my leg. 'Or maybe you hungry? You all skin-and-bones.' I've no idea where he'd heard that expression: it certainly won't have been anyone talking about Charlie because he's 'built to last', as Granny says.

'Right, that's it,' said the crotchety, skinny, stinky assistant. 'I'm calling –'

But she didn't get chance to call anyone, because she was interrupted by a store announcement.

'Donna Trout to the tills please, Donna Trout to the tills.'

Charlie and I sniggered. Dad once called Mum a silly old trout when she forgot to pack his trunks for a trip to the seaside. She said that was rude, and made him wear his pants for swimming, say sorry 14 times and wipe Charlie's bottom for a week. (He didn't wipe it non-stop, only when he'd had a poo.)

'I… You… Grr!' Shouty Trouty screeched in frustration. 'Don't even think of going into that display! You won't get away with it, you know! I'll be watching you!' she said, stabbing her stained, yellow finger towards a security camera before stomping off.

How rude. Charlie and I looked at each other and shrugged.

'I think you're right,' I said. 'Miss Trout needs her lunch.'

Charlie stepped up into the bathroom.

'You're not supposed to be up there,' I said. 'Trout Face said so.'

'I not like the fishy woman,' said Charlie and I couldn't disagree with that, so I joined him.

I ran my hands across the wall of boiled sweet tiles. 'These would look amazing in my bedroom.'

I heard a straining nose, and looked round to see Charlie holding the edge of the toilet, his face creased up in concentration. (He wasn't sitting on it; he doesn't need to, because he's still in nappy pants. He's too old for nappy pants now really, but Mum says she can't face potty training yet, and Dad says he's very busy at work.)

'No!' he said.

I knew what was coming next.

'Don't. Look. At. Me!'

He grunted and went purple. He looked like he was trying to push the sink right through the wall.

'Harry! DON'T LOOK AT ME!'

I'd seen it all before, anyway. I turned to look in the mirrored tiles; my freckles were nearly joined up in some places now. I wondered if it was possible to turn completely brown, then I'd be just like my best friend Chantelle.

After another minute of huffing and puffing, Charlie finally breathed out with a 'whoosh'.

'We go find Mummy and Daddy?' he said chirpily. 'Is a bit smelly in here.'

He was right; it was the kind of pong that you only get on a pig farm, or at our house.

And so I walked in search of Mum and Dad, and Charlie waddled.

We found them in the end, holding two tiles side by side; one cream, one brown and both very, very boring.

'Yes, I think that'll work,' said Mum. 'Grab the cards, let's order them. Oh, hello you two!'

Dad swept Charlie up into his arms. 'Whaddya

reckon? They cost an arm and a leg, but they're smart, eh?'

'It's OK, I suppose,' I said. 'But we found much better ones.'

Charlie looked down at the two tiles. 'That one porridge... and that one's poo,' he said, pointing.

'Oh brilliant,' said Mum. 'Now I won't be able to cook a meal without thinking about porridge and... the other one.' She wrinkled her nose. 'Talking of which... could you give him a sniff, Tom?'

Dad twirled Charlie over and stuck his nose into Charlie's bottom. 'Strike a light,' he said, coughing and spluttering. 'I think this one's cooked.'

'Your turn,' said Mum, holding out the change bag. 'Definitely your turn.'

'I done poo-poo in the bathroom!' said Charlie, proudly.

Mummy shot me a look. 'He didn't. Tell me he didn't.'

'Nah,' I said. 'Well he was *in* the bathroom, but he didn't do it on the toilet.'

'Shame,' said Dad. 'I thought he might have potty trained himself for a moment. Come on then, let's get out of here. Harry, you grab this stuff, I'll bring the stinkbomb.' He handed me some catalogues and the tile cards he'd chosen and we headed to the service desk.

Guess who was on the service desk? The Trout, of course.

'Did you find everything you were looking for?' she said to Mum and Dad, nice as pie.

Dad turned to Mum. 'Yes, I think so, didn't we love? All good to go?'

Fishy Finger's nose twitched. Charlie was still being held at each end like a plank of stinky wood by Dad, and she looked at him with disgust. Charlie looked directly at her, and I put my hand on his back just to show I was on his side.

'Ah yes, sorry about the smell. As soon as we order the tiles, we'll get this little horror out of your hair.'

The Troutster instinctively put her hands to her thin, dry hair. It looked like hay. If I ever get lost in the desert, that's how I expect my hair would look.

'Well, I won't get him out of *your* hair,' said Dad, 'that would be disgusting! Eh?' Dad read the name from her name badge. 'Eh, Donna, whaddya reckon?'

'Can I have the tiles you've chosen and your quantity please,' she said, holding out a wizened hand and looking like she'd just discovered lemons.

'Suit yourself,' said Dad. 'I think you've got the cards, haven't you Liz?'

'Nope,' said Mum, who was on her phone. 'You picked them up.'

'Hang on... Harry, can you take Charlie for second. Don't let him go anywhere or sit down, whatever you do.'

I put the catalogues and cards on the floor and took Charlie. I can *just* about carry him now, for about two minutes, but I wasn't very keen – the smell was horrendous.

'Now then, I must have them here somewhere...' Dad started pulling receipts, tissues and other rubbish out of his jeans pockets.

'Come on Tom, you had them just now,' said Mum, sorting through the bits and bobs on the counter.

'Yeah I know, it's weird. They'll be here somewhere, I'm sure.'

Two minutes was up: I couldn't hold Charlie any longer. I let him slip down until he was standing on his feet, but he didn't like that and wriggled out of my grip.

Mum had left her phone on the counter – unlocked. So I started a game of Diamond Dazzler while I waited, but there was no reception so I couldn't connect. I played around with the camera, taking selfies and slo-mo video.

Dad gave up. 'Nope, I can't find them. We wanted the square cream ones?' said Dad.

The Trout Monster raised her eyebrow and pointed to a warehouse full of tiles. 'I'm afraid we're not trained in mind reading, sir.'

Dad sighed. 'Fair enough. I'll get another card.'

But before he could say anything else, Charlie chipped in.

'I get them! I get them!'

'Charlie! Charlie!' But it was too late: Charlie was off. Except he wasn't running. Instead he bent down, tucked his head halfway under, and flopped over. I'd call it a forward roll, but then you'd think he'd gone forwards, when actually he flopped sideways. A couple of cards, a rubber and a bottle opener fell out of his dungarees pocket.

He looked around, corrected himself, and then rolled in the direction of the tiles: bend, tuck, flop.

15

That was as far as he got before Mum pinned him to the ground. 'Oh Charlie, it's gone *everywhere*!' she said.

I didn't need to ask what she meant. Once, at school, the naughty boys blocked up their toilets with toilet roll and a dictionary. They did it on Friday and nobody found out until Monday and by then the toilets had overflowed all into the playground and Mr Jones was *livid* (that's a word I learned from our WOW words board). Anyway, the smell was terrible, the same as it was now.

'Where are your toilets, please?' Mum asked Fish Face.

'Sorry, we don't have customer toilets.'

'OK... could we use your staff toilet then? I'm afraid it's a bit of an emergency.' Mum smiled.

'I'm afraid that staff toilets are only for staff. There's a McDonald's down the road, they have toilets.'

'No, but seriously... ' Mum looked at her. 'You're serious, aren't you?'

'I'm afraid that staff toilets are restricted to staff only, madam. It's Health and Safety.'

'Ah well,' said Dad, finally springing into action. 'We'll just change him here then.' And he unzipped the change bag and pulled out a mat, nappy and wipes.

'No, sir, you can't do that!' exclaimed the Trout Lout. 'That's really not acceptable!'

'Too late,' said Dad. He'd shoved Mum out of the way and was now stripping Charlie down. Now Dad doesn't change Charlie as much as Mum; he says he does, but he doesn't. If he did, he'd know that there's good news, because Charlie doesn't wear babygrows, or shout and scream any more. But there's bad news, because Charlie doesn't lie on his back like a baby any more either.

I was filming this bit now. Dad won't let me start a vlog because he says his movie star days are over. I said that nobody would want to watch a movie about anyone as boring as him anyway, and he clomped me on the head with a bag of onions. Anyway, when he does let me start a vlog, this was definitely going on it.

The dungarees came off first, and the smell increased by about a billion times. The customers behind us in the queue pulled funny faces and decided they needed to look at some more tiles. Dad peered inside the dungarees, and looked away as if he'd seen a terrible monster from the

17

deep, which he probably had.

'I'll sort this one,' he said to Mum. 'Look, here are those bloomin' cards,' he said, picking them up. 'You just order the tiles and let's get out of here. We need seven square metres of the cream, and five of the brown, if it's not too much *trouble*,' he said up to the counter. He spoke the last few words as if he's accidentally eaten a bit of whatever was inside Charlie's dungarees, and handed the tile cards up to Mum, who passed them over to the Trout Trollop. She took them without a word, and started tapping away on her keyboard.

'This top's going to have to come off,' mumbled Dad, yanking at Charlie's t-shirt. That left him standing in his saggy, baggy nappy pants, legs apart and hands in the air, as if an armed robber had walked into the changing rooms at a preschool. Dad ripped off his nappy: right there, in the middle of the store. He was facing me, so I couldn't see what was going on down near his bottom, although Dad's face suggested it wasn't pretty.

'Why did you do roly-polys, Charlie?' I asked him, still filming.

'Coz Daddy said I not sit down,' said Charlie.

'Fair enough,' I said. Mum shook her head and

stood at the counter, holding her credit card.

'Is there a problem?' said Mum.

The Trouty One paused. She looked at her screen, and then down at Charlie who was now bending over with his hands on the floor.

'What was the quantity again?' she said.

'Seven cream, five brown,' grunted Dad.

'That granny and grandad are upside down froo my bottom,' said Charlie, peering at an elderly couple who were trying not to look, but couldn't help it.

The Terrible Trout shuddered, and turned back to her keyboard.

'That'll be £473.50 please,' she said with a sudden smile.

'That's more than I thought,' said Mum. 'Are you sure that's right?'

'It's probably the VAT or something,' said Dad. He'd now got a clean nappy on Charlie, and was rifling through the change bag for clean clothes. 'Let's just go for it.'

With another smile, Trout Pout snatched the credit card from Mum and shoved it into the machine. 'They'll be ready for collection in seven to ten working days, madam. We look forward to seeing you again then.' She held out the receipt and Mum's card with a snaggle-toothed smile. Imagine if Year 1 had to make a model of Stonehenge out of old cheddar cheese, and then all the stones started falling over on the way home. That's what her teeth looked like.

'Sadly we won't able to make it,' said Dad standing up. He was holding Charlie, who was now wearing swimming trunks and a Peppa Pig vest. 'We'll be on holiday. Our builder will pick them up for us. It would have been so lovely to experience your customer service again.'

'Phone,' said Mum, holding out her hand to me.

'Bag,' said Dad, pointing at the change bag.

'Car', said Charlie, pointing to the exit.

And we left.

Dad was right, because that weekend we travelled up to spend a week with my Granny. She lives one hundred or two hundred miles away or something like that, and she needed help with her shed so Dad went to fix it, and we all went with him.

'I can't wait to get away from this dust,' said Mum as we set off. 'I just hope Jim has it all under control.'

Jim is a builder who lives down the road. And for weeks he'd been drinking tea while his men dug up our garden, leaning on cement mixers while they built walls, and hooting the horn of his battered white van when he saw us walking back from school. At the end of it we were going to have a new kitchen.

It was Friday afternoon when we left. His men had gone home, leaving Jim sitting on the floor surrounded by bits of kitchen cabinet and instruction manuals.

'It's been made faulty, it's got the wrong bits,' he said to Dad, rotating a half-built cupboard. 'There's no end panel. You'll need to order a new one. We could be a week late finishing with this delay.'

'It can't be faulty,' muttered Dad, picking up spare bits of cupboard, turning them over and putting them down.

I put down my rucksack and looked at the instructions. They were a bit like the ones for my Marble Run; no words, but just pictures. If you make sure it looks the same, it's easy.

'That's a bit old for you, missy,' said Jim when he saw me. 'Probably best you don't touch anything, leave it to the experts.'

I looked at his cupboard.

'You've got that piece on backwards,' I said.

'Like I say, best you butt out, eh?' said Jim.

'But you haven't done it right. That's why you can't find your end panel.'

'Now look, this is quite hard enough –'

'She's right, Jim,' said Dad, holding the instructions up to the cupboard. 'You've just got it on back to front. Nice work, Hatster,' Dad said, squeezing my shoulder.

Jim huffed, and grabbed the instructions, before huffing some more. 'Bloomin' kids, shouldn't be allowed anywhere near.'

'So anyway, like I was saying. They should ring me on Monday about the tiles, and I'll drop you a text to say they're ready to pick up.'

'Right you are,' said Jim, banging a piece into place with a hammer. Dad winced. 'Are you sure that's the right way to … ' Jim scowled at him. 'Never mind. They're all paid for, should be straightforward – two different designs.'

'Two designs? You never mentioned that. Could cost a bit extra. How do you want them?'

Dad sighed. 'I don't know. We were just thinking you could do them mixed up, you know, random. There's more of one than the other.'

'Sounds complicated,' said Jim.

'It's not,' said Dad.

'Sounds it.'

'It isn't,' I added.

'Didn't ask you,' said Jim.

'OK you two, enough,' said Dad. 'I'm sure you'll do the right thing. Call me if there are any problems.'

'Well that's not *exactly* what we agreed.' Dad was on the phone in Granny's kitchen as we ate breakfast. He was walking up and down, occasionally stopping to drum his fingers on the table and make faces at Mum.

'I guess we can live with it, Jim, but it's not ideal,' Dad continued. 'It doesn't sound like we've got any choice, to be honest.' There was a pause while Dad listened.

'What? What?' Mum whispered.

Dad covered the phone with his hand. 'He's put the door in the wrong place.'

'WHAT?' Mum nearly shouted. Granny looked up from the hob, where she was stirring the porridge.

'It's done now,' Dad whispered. 'Hole knocked through, door put – oh, yes, I'm still here, Jim. Just explaining to Liz. She's fine with it.'

Mum threw a teatowel at Dad's head. He ducked.

'OK, what about the tiles? … Good, glad that went OK. You didn't get served by that old boot did you, the fish-faced woman? … Count yourself lucky, she's a right grump… Yes, I'm glad you like the tiles, they should be nice, they cost enough… Well I guess so, I hadn't really thought of them as bright, but I suppose you're right. Anyway, we love them too.'

Mum raised her eyebrows at Dad, but he ignored her.

'That's right, we want tiles from the floor to ceiling on the end wall please, then just put them under the kitchen units everywhere else… Just put the dark ones wherever they look good. No, I'm sure it'll look great… Yep, OK then. No, no need to send a photo, I trust you. Yep, bye… bye. Bye.'

Dad put the phone on the table and sighed. 'I don't know why I said that. I don't trust him an inch.'

'He's got the right amount of tiles, and you've told him exactly where you want them,' said Mum. 'Surely even he can't muck that up?'

Mum was right, of course. Jim did exactly as he had been told, as we saw when we stumbled into the new kitchen late on Sunday night to see how far they'd got. Charlie had fallen asleep in the car so he was in a filthy mood, and Mum and Dad weren't much better.

Dad flicked on the new lights and… well we nearly had to switch them off again. We held our hands to our eyes as if we were looking straight into the sun. We had walked into our very own disco: a glittering, shimmering room of mirrors, a kaleidoscope of colour. Spotlights under the new kitchen cabinets were reflected and coloured by the mirrored walls, casting blue, red, pink and yellow shadows across the work surface. Opposite, mirrored and coloured tiles stretched from floor to ceiling, just like Dad had asked (sort of). And reflected in the tiles we could see a family, mouths wide open in astonishment.

For a moment, nobody said a word.

'Whoah,' I said.

'You can say that again,' said Dad quietly.

'Whoah!' said Charlie.

'Tell me it's a dream. Tell me I'm going to wake up,' said Mum.

'Is not a dream, is REAL!' shouted Charlie, running into the middle of the room and spinning around in delight.

'It's absolutely awesome,' I said. 'I can't believe you chose these tiles.'

'WE DIDN'T!' yelled Mum and Dad at exactly the same time.

I looked at them.

'We didn't! Why would we choose these? I've never even seen them! How could we… ' Mum paused. 'Tom, when you handed the cards to me in the shop, did you check them?'

'Well no, of course not, I was busy hosing down our youngest child, remember? Did you?'

'Well no, I just handed them over. I thought…' Mum trailed off again.

'That *woman!*' growled Dad.

'What, the fishy one?' I said.

'Yes, very fishy indeed. She must have known! Why would we be ordering disco tiles? We said they were brown and cream!'

'I LOVE da disco tiles!' said Charlie, who was literally bouncing off the walls in delight.

'I have a feeling this isn't going to end well,' said Dad. 'But I tell you what. By the time I've finished, that Donna Trout is going to wish she'd let us use her toilet.'

Dad was hardly off the phone during the next week. It seemed Mum and Dad didn't want to keep the tiles – in fact they wanted them removed as soon as possible, which was a bit of a spoil-sport thing to do.

Jim came round, and went away grumbling about how he said he could have sent a photo, but Dad had said no.

Charlie and I got quizzed like prisoners, and

we explained that yes of course we'd seen the disco tiles, and yes of course Charlie had picked up the cards but then he'd picked up lots of cards, and no we didn't have a clue how they ended up in Dad's hand.

Mr Philips from the tile company came round. Stuffed into a suit with a bright red face, at first he couldn't stop chortling. He said in his opinion it looked really 'modern' and 'groovy', and had we thought about keeping it? That got my hopes up, but Mum dashed them again straight away by telling him that nobody had said 'groovy' for 38 years and that he shouldn't be so silly, what did he think she was, a fifteen-year-old girl?

But then he got all serious, and said that of course they accept returns, but not when they've been stuck on the wall. And he could offer us a 5% discount on a new order if we liked, just because he was feeling generous. 'Generous?' said Dad, 'well if that's generous I'd hate to hear what you offer when you're feeling stingy.'

He didn't like that and very soon he left, without even eating his digestive biscuit. Charlie ate it instead.

That evening we were all in the lounge. We'd had our stories, done our teeth and were all ready for bed. Dad and Mum were stretched out on the sofa and weren't nagging us to get upstairs so Charlie and I played quietly, hoping they'd forget us. Charlie was trying to turn his nose inside out, and I was playing on Mum's phone.

'I just don't understand,' said Mum. 'We might have got the cards mixed up, but that old ratbag *knew* we wanted cream and brown tiles. And if she didn't, she definitely should have checked when we ordered tiles for a lunatic asylum. She knew exactly what she was doing, I reckon.'

Dad just shook his head despondently.

'It's going to cost us thousands,' said Mum.

Why did you do roly-polys, Charlie?

That voice was mine: I'd found the video of Charlie getting changed on Mum's phone. Charlie tottered across to watch, and we screamed with laughter. 'Look at Dad's face! You can almost smell it through the phone!'

What was the quantity again?

That was Donna Trout, being miserable.

'Hang on, I'll find the bit where Charlie bends over,' I said.

'Wait a minute,' said Dad, suddenly sitting up. 'Let me have a look at that.'

I took the phone across and we huddled round. We watched as Mum stood with her credit card held out. *Is there a problem?* she had said.

From where I'd been filming at the side of the counter we could see Charlie, Dad, Mum and Donna Trout – and we also had a very good view of Donna Trout's computer screen.

'Just pause it right there,' said Dad, taking the phone. 'Let's have a closer look at that,' he said, zooming right in. There, on the screen, it said:

CUSTOMER ORDER:

MIRROR TILES
QUANTITY REQUIRED (SQ M): 7

DISCO COLOUR TILES
QUANTITY REQUIRED (SQ M): 5

'They're even *called* disco tiles!' said Mum.

'Yes! And listen,' said Dad. 'Just listen to what I said before.'

Dad scrubbed back to the bit when he was changing Charlie.

We need seven square metres of the cream, and five of the brown, if it's not too much trouble.

'Well well,' said Mum. 'That miserable boot knew exactly what she was doing!'

'I think I'll be giving Mr Philips another call first thing in the morning,' said Dad. He pulled me onto his lap. 'And do you know, thanks to our little screen warrior here, I think we might have a boring cream and brown kitchen after all.'

There was a sniff, and then a wail. Charlie started crying. You can't please everyone.

'So my video saved you, right?' I said. I saw an opportunity, and I was going to go for it.

'Yes, do you know, I think it did,' said Dad.

'So… does that mean I can start my vlog?' Dad pushed me off, and piled cushions on top of me. But he didn't say no.

Church

'It's a family service,' said Granny Fran. 'I'm sure you'll be good as gold, won't you Charlie?'

Charlie looked up at Granny. 'Fnugh figgin gurnle,' he said, or something like that. It was hard to tell because he had his whole fist in his mouth. I didn't know you could do that, and I'm not sure Charlie did either because his eyes were sticking out and had gone all boggly like a mudskipper.

'I'm not sure it's a good idea,' said Mum. 'Last time we went to church he walked down the aisle in the middle of the service and asked the vicar to stop being so boring.'

'You can't blame him, I often feel like doing the same thing,' said Dad, pulling Charlie's fist out of his mouth. It was covered in dribble. 'I've got a good idea. Why don't I take Charlie to the café or something, while you guys go and be all holy? I don't mind.'

'I'll bet you wouldn't,' said Mum. 'No chance. There's no way Harry and I are sitting there while you eat bacon sandwiches. That settles it, we're all going.'

We could already hear the bells because the church is just round the corner from Granny Fran's house. We hardly ever go when we're back home but Granny goes all the time because she doesn't have much to do. All the old people go there. I think they just like sitting down in the dark.

We were already wearing smart clothes because it was Easter but Mum made us brush our hair and everything. By the time Dad had wiped the strawberry jam out of Charlie's curly locks, and then lost him when he ran away screaming, and then found him behind the compost heap, we were late. Granny was standing at the door with her walking stick looking stern, which is what she does a lot these days.

Have you noticed that about old people? I'm not sure it's their fault. I think it's because the skin goes all saggy like wet washing, and then they're not strong enough to pull it into the right shape to make a smile. Or maybe some old people are just more grumpy.

'He needs firm boundaries, Elizabeth,' said Granny. Mum didn't say anything, but she did grunt a bit: she was dragging Charlie by his arms towards the door. Charlie stuck out his legs and hooked his feet around the front door frame. Granny tutted. 'You've been too soft on him for too long.'

Mum ignored her, blew the hair out of her eyes and looked up at me. 'Harry, you know what to do.'

I did. I grabbed his feet and we set off for church carrying Charlie like a plank of wood. And as usual, as soon as we started walking and Charlie swung to and fro, screams turned to giggles and everything was OK again.

The sun was shining, I didn't have to go back to school for another week, and Granny had promised me we could do some baking after church. I was happy.

Old people were crawling towards the church from every direction. (They weren't actually crawling, that's just a story word I used. But they were going *very* slowly, like toys that are running out of battery. It looked like some of them might not even make it.)

'Merry Easter!' shouted Charlie.

Most of them said 'Happy Easter!' back, and some of them even found enough strength for a little wave. Granny started chatting to everybody. Lots of the old women were wearing fancy hats and wearing dresses the same colour as those rubbish gel pens, like light blue, pale yellow, and that pink colour that looks like it should be perfect for faces but you can hardly even see on the paper. I couldn't see any other children, which was a worrying sign.

At the door, a woman with a kind smile and whiskers on her chin gave Charlie a bag of pencils and pictures to colour in. 'Fank you,' he said very nicely, before turning to Mum. 'Why is that woman's chin –'

But Charlie didn't get any further, because Mum clapped her hand over his mouth and lifted him up. We shuffled down the aisle and found an empty pew. Charlie sat on the floor and sang Jingle Bells, Granny twisted and turned to talk to her friends, and I slid my bottom up and down the shiny wooden seats.

'Hey, what's happened to Mrs Mozart?' whispered Dad to Mum. 'I only come here for the music.'

Dad was joking. In Granny's church the music is normally terrible. I mean properly awful. The organ is played by Mrs Hughes; that's one of Granny's neighbours who is very good at looking grumpy, but flabbergastingly bad at playing the organ. You can usually see her up on her stool, thumping on the keys like she's *Little Rabbit Foo Foo*, trying to bop mice on the head.

But this time the seat was empty and proper orchestra music was coming from the speakers. It was in tune, and quite nice actually.

'I'm not sure where she's gone,' whispered Mum. She nudged Granny and pointed at the empty stool. 'What's happened to Val?'

'She's broken her arm,' said Granny.

'Ooh, that's terrible,' said Mum.

'Yes, really very terrible,' said Dad. Mum kicked his leg.

'She was out on her bicycle and saw Jimmy the postman dropping rubber bands,' explained Granny. 'You know how she hates litter, so she started shaking her fists and crashed into a tree.

And since nobody else can play the organ, we have to use CDs instead. Just until we can find someone who can play like her.'

'Have you tried asking at the zoo? One of the monkeys might help you out,' said Dad brightly. But Granny gave him one of her looks, just as the vicar raised her hands for quiet. The music faded and everyone hushed.

Well, not quite everyone: Charlie had just got to his favourite bit of his favourite Christmas song. And like always, he sang it at the top of his voice: 'Jingle all da way, HEY!'

'Welcome, everyone, to this special *Easter* service!' The vicar smiled towards us and held her hands out wide, her white robes flowing.

Charlie pulled himself to his feet using my dress as a handle and clambered up onto Dad's lap to find out who was speaking.

'Oof!' whispered Dad as Charlie trod all over his lap to get a better view.

'I can't see!' said Charlie.

Dad lifted him up a bit so he could see.

'Still nuffink!' said Charlie, so Dad lifted him high into the air like a football trophy.

'At this joyful time of year it's so heartening to see a few new faces,' the vicar continued.

'Why is God wearing a dress?' announced Charlie loudly. A few people laughed, lots tutted, and the old woman in front of Charlie made a choking noise.

'Shh!' said Mum, pulling Charlie out of Dad's grasp. But he wriggled away and slid back down onto the floor as the vicar burbled on and on. Eventually we stood up to sing a song I didn't know, and neither did Dad by the sound of it. Mum can sing OK but Dad's voice is awful. You know the noise it makes when your mum tries to suck up a sock with a vacuum cleaner? It sounds like that. Granny didn't even need the words, and Charlie just went 'la, la, la,' whenever he felt like it.

Time for the first prayer, and there was a problem: Charlie had arranged all the cushions in a row and was lying on them, so we had nothing to kneel on.

'Shh, I sleeping!' he said, opening his eyes a little and grinning. I don't remember when I first learned how to whisper, but Charlie definitely doesn't know how yet. Granny gave Mum another look and bowed her head.

For a while, it was quiet: singing, prayers, talking, singing, prayers, talking. Stand up, sit down, stand up, sit down: after a while I couldn't tell if I was awake or asleep it was so boring. Charlie was colouring in; he'd complained that he only had brown and black crayons left, but that's because he'd poked the other ones through the holes in the metal grates in the floor. That earned him another stern look from Granny which he ignored as he scribbled on the back of the pictures he was supposed to be using.

Dad was bored too, I could tell. He kept squeezing my hand, or picking at fluff on his jumper, or flicking through the pages of the hymn book, probably because he liked the noise.

'Daddy,' said Charlie, pulling on his arm. 'Look what I done!' This was in the middle of another lecture. Or a prayer. Or maybe it was a reading. One of those.

'Daddy! Daddy! DADDY!'

I saw a couple of heads twitch in front of us and gave Dad a nudge. Dad looked down at my brother, who was holding up his drawing. 'Oh, that's… nice. Very colourful,' said Dad as quietly as he could. 'What is it?'

Why do grown-ups tell lies when they tell us not to? If you think of colourful, you probably think of a rainbow, or maybe a bag of Skittles. But this wasn't colourful: it was a muddy, browny splodge, a nest of grumpy scribbles that filled the paper.

Daddy reached out to take it, but Charlie pulled it away and scowled. 'Is not for you,' he hissed. 'Is for Mummy.' He smiled again. 'Do you like it?'

'Yes I do, my little chubbablub, but what is it?'

'Is a drawing, you silly billy,' said Charlie.

You have to remember that all this time there were only two people talking in this big, dark church: a man at the front doing the reading, and Charlie. Oh and Dad, but he was quite quiet. Every time Charlie spoke the man stopped talking and restarted his sentence. He kept frowning, as if he couldn't quite believe he was being interrupted, especially by somebody he couldn't even see. I could tell that Mum was getting ants in her pants, because she kept shuffling and looking at Dad.

Now then, I'm going to stop this story to tell you something I've just remembered. It's a story inside a story, like a toy inside a chocolate egg.

Once upon a time Granny came to stay, and we lost the remote control. This doesn't sound very interesting, I know, but don't give up yet.

It was just after Granny had been donked on the leg by a silly car going too fast, and she was taken to hospital in an ambulance. When they let her out she came to stay with us so she could eat all our chocolate biscuits and tell Mum how naughty Charlie is. Anyway Mum helped her out of the car and into the lounge, and plonked her down on the sofa.

Charlie and I were watching something on YouTube about car crashes; I didn't mean to watch it, it just came up when I was looking for Harry Potter.

'That's really not very suitable for children,' said Granny.

'Goodness me,' said Dad, 'I don't know how they got that on the telly. We never normally let you watch stuff like that, do we?'

'Yes you do,' I said.

'Well hardly ever,' said Dad, looking around

41

for the remote.

'Just every morning before school,' I said.

'Yes, quite,' said Dad. 'Now where is that wretched thing… '

'And every day after school. And weekends.'

'Never mind that, Harry, help me out. Turn that rubbish off,' said Dad. 'All those accidents, they're probably giving your granny flashbacks.'

I looked around for the remote control, but I couldn't see it either.

'TURN IT OFF, Harry!' said Mum.

At least I think that's what she said. It was hard to tell because the noise from the telly was drowning her out. Crash, bang, scrunch: a car on screen smashed straight through a shop window, as if it didn't know where the door was. Meanwhile the green volume bars were going up and up, louder and louder.

'Harry! The telly!' That was Dad again, who was now shouting to get himself heard.

'I CAN'T FIND THE REMOTE!' I yelled back, picking up cushions and looking under the table.

Charlie yelled something too, but all I could see was his mouth moving because the telly was now at full bars, maximum volume. Engines revved, sirens wailed and people were shouting in funny languages. Granny sat on the sofa with her hands over her ears, looking straight forward like she wished she was still being run over by a car.

'WHERE. IS. THE. REMOTE?' shouted Mum, trying to do sign language like a headteacher in assembly. For the 'remote' bit she even pointed her hand at the telly and pressed imaginary buttons on it. As if that would work.

'I. DON'T. KNOW!' I screamed back. By now Mum and me were running around, throwing things on the floor and pushing our hands between the sofa cushions. Dad was fiddling around with the back of the telly, trying to find some buttons that might turn the sound down. Charlie was running round and round the coffee table, screaming with joy. And Granny now looked like we could give her a chocolate biscuit every minute for the rest of her life and it still wouldn't be enough, even with a glass of Coke.

Finally, Granny couldn't stand it any more: she grabbed hold of the arms of the chair and tried to pull herself to her feet. As she did so the telly got quieter again, even though a monster truck was smashing into a wall.

'Mum!' said Mum, rushing across the room. 'You can't get up on your own!'

It didn't matter anyway because Granny wasn't strong enough, and sank back down again. Up went the volume, right back to the 'So Loud It's Scary' setting.

Mum grabbed her arms and Dad came over too, and started pushing his hand under her bottom.

'Thomas!' barked Granny. 'Get off me!'

But Dad didn't stop: push, push he went, all the way round, like he was tucking in a sheet. Finally, with a huge grin on his face, he pulled out the missing remote control from under her bum and pressed the off button. There was a moment's silence.

'Try that once more and I shall *never* come to this house again,' said Granny crossly.

Daddy raised his eyebrows and smiled before handing me the remote and leaving the room.

Right, we're back in the proper story. Don't get confused. I told you that bit because I just thought of it, and if I didn't tell you now I might forget.

So Charlie showed his picture to Dad, and called him a silly billy. Remember?

'I *know* it's a drawing,' whispered Dad, 'and it's very good, but what have you drawn? What is it? What have you done, my little rinkidink?'

When Charlie answered it was at a top-of-the-tree, right-across-the-valley-and-back-again volume. Louder than the telly when your Granny is sitting on the remote control. So loud I bet the skeletons in the graveyard outside tried covered their bony ears with their bony hands. Charlie's words dropped into a tiny gap in the man's boring speech.

'I. DONE. A. POO!'

'What?' said Mum, who had finally realised she couldn't ignore him any longer, probably because everyone in the church was now looking round. She grabbed the change bag and snatched Charlie up into her arms. He still had his drawing, and was waving it around.

'Look at my massif poo!' shouted Charlie as Mum lifted him high into the air, waving his piece of paper. 'Is brown! Is squidgy! Is not stinky though!'

Mum barged past, muttering to Dad that she'd just have to change Charlie herself then since Dad obviously couldn't be bothered, and this was all very embarrassing, and this was absolutely the last time we came to church.

'No, no!' Dad said, grabbing at Mum's jumper. 'It's not a real poo!'

But it was too late: Mum was gone. The man at the front had stopped talking and as Mum marched down the aisle everyone turned their heads, just like they would at the world's slowest tennis match. Charlie waved his poo flag and looked very happy at all the attention.

'She's going to kill you,' I said to Dad quietly, as we pretended we didn't know them.

'What d'ya mean? How was that my fault?' said Dad. He paused. 'You're right, she will.'

I wasn't wrong: Mum was definitely going to kill him. She came back during the next hymn, dumping Charlie on the floor.

'Nice walk?' said Dad between verses, smiling.

'He said he'd done a poo!' she whispered.

'Ooh I am cross. Why didn't you tell me?'

'He did *sort-of* tell you,' I said, though I'm not sure that helped.

'I tried to say something, but you left so quickly I thought maybe you needed a poo yourself,' said Dad.

'I've never been so embarrassed in all my life,' said Mum, trying to find the right hymn in the book.

'Are you sure?' said Dad. 'What about that time on the ferry? Or in the hospital? Or at the animal park? Or at the soft play? Or –'

'Zip it,' said Mum. She closed her eyes, raised her face to the ceiling and launched into the chorus with enthusiasm.

Except the hymn had just ended and everyone sat down, leaving her singing on her own.

Even her own mum – that's my Granny – was embarrassed by that. And since a funny look wasn't going to work this time, Granny dragged Mum down into her seat instead. Mum sat with a ketchup red face, looking like she was dreaming of ways to disappear into the centre of the earth, or murder Dad, or maybe both, while Dad and I tried not to laugh.

A few minutes later and it was time for another prayer. I dropped to my knees. Ouch! My kneecaps clonked onto the wooden floor – my bright pink kneeler, the cushion I'd been using, had gone. I peered along the row, and Mum and Dad were looking around, too, but that was for a different reason: Charlie had also vanished. Checking that Granny's eyes were tightly shut, Mum pointed underneath the pews; she wanted me to look.

I lowered myself to the floor and had a peek. From here I could see I could see a million ankles and shoes, walking sticks and handbags – and a forest of kneelers, too. They were either on the floor or hanging from their little hooks on the backs of the pews. Charlie was nowhere to be seen. But just as I was about to give up a chubby and rather grubby hand, like a sausage on a stick, appeared about three rows further forward. And as I watched, this hand slowly unhooked a bright green cushion and lifted it out of sight.

And that wasn't the end of it. Next to the cushion was an open purple handbag. The hand came within touching distance, and then disappeared. But then it was back, hovering at the entrance of the bag. You could almost *see* the hand thinking, which is about the most stupid thing I've ever written.

But then the hand obviously thought, 'why not?', dipped into the handbag and pulled out a fistful of brightly wrapped sweets.

I got back up to my seat and had a look. The pew where Charlie was causing mischief was half empty, with just an old couple sitting at one end. They both had crazy white hair, and the man had a hearing aid as big as an iPhone. Talking of crazy hair, every now and again I could just see a wisp of Charlie's mop bobbing along the row, and I elbowed Mum. She craned her neck, and elbowed Dad. He grinned and went to elbow Granny, but then decided against it.

'And now,' said the vicar, 'please stand for our next hymn. That's number 565 on your sheets, *Come down, O Love Divine*.'

Have you ever seen that trick where someone hides behind a sofa or a wall, and pretends to walk downstairs by bending their knees with every step? And then they pretend to walk back up again? If you haven't, find your Mum or Dad right now, and get them to show you. It's brilliant, and I'll wait. If they say they won't do it, get yourself a better Mum or Dad. (I'M JOKING. Unless you want to swap them, of course.)

OK, are you back? It's great, isn't it? Well for a second that's what I thought Charlie was doing because up, up, up he came, higher and higher with every step, holding an upside-down hymn book out in front of him. Except that there weren't any steps in that pew, and he was now higher than the old man, who looked up in surprise before smiling broadly.

'Charlie!' said Dad as loudly as he dared over the music, and Charlie looked round. He was chewing – probably a toffee by the way he was concentrating. I love toffees, don't you? They definitely help you think. They should give them out in maths lessons.

Charlie didn't look very steady way up there, and when I climbed up on my pew I saw why. He had made a staircase out of the kneelers and was now teetering on the very top.

Granny had seen Charlie now and it's safe to say she was hopping mad, or she would have been if she could hop, which she can't any more. 'Get him down!' she urged Mum, before returning to her singing.

'I can't get to him!' she said. 'Tom, get him down!'

Dad turned to Mum with his eyebrows raised, then looked at me. He reached forward, but there was no way his arms were long enough. 'Any bright ideas?'

'I'll get him,' I said. I sidled out of the pew and nipped forward. I kneeled on the first cushion step.

'Psst! Psst! Charlie!' I whispered up to him. 'Mummy says you have to come down!'

Charlie looked down and grinned. He dropped the hymn book which bounced down the steps. Then he reached into his trouser pocket and pulled out two toffees.

'You wan one, Harry?'

I definitely did, but he was so far away he might as well have been at the top of Mount Everest.

'Come down! Now! You're in big trouble!'

Charlie shook his head. I'd have to fetch him.

So up I went. The first couple of steps were OK because they only took me as high as the seat, but after that it started getting very wobbly, and there was nothing to hold on to. I looked across to Dad, who waved me upwards, and Mum, who put her hand over her face. Granny pretended she couldn't see me.

'Charlie! Come ON!'

I reached out towards him, but he wasn't looking at me; he was trying to get the wrapper off his next toffee. It was one of those ones that's twisted on and he was going quite pink with the effort.

The hymn ended and everyone sat down, which left Charlie high up in the sky on his own.

'I don't think that's a good idea, little one,' said the vicar from the pulpit. 'I think maybe –'

Who knows what the vicar thought. Who cares what the vicar thought. Because Charlie's time at the top was over. He was so busy concentrating on his toffee wrapper that he stepped right off his towering pile of cushions. The congregation gasped as he waved his arms around, trying to get his balance. One lady screamed.

In fact the only person taking no notice was the old man next to him, who was staring into space with a smile on his face. But maybe he should have been watching, because Charlie was toppling straight into his lap.

But here's a thing: the man glanced up and simply held out his arms, and Charlie fell straight into them.

'Charlie!' he exclaimed, tipping him upright. 'Hello sailor!'

The old man yanked out his hearing aid and we heard a hundred people say stuff like, *Phew!*, *That was lucky!* and *The parent of that child must be an idiot*.

'Hello Gerry Tricks!' said Charlie. And it was only then that I recognised him: it was the crazy guy from the hospital. If you haven't read about that in the first book of Charlie stories – and without spoiling it for you – Charlie ends up eating secret snacks with a man called Mr Jamieson in the TV room at Granny's hospital. Oops, I just told you the ending. Anyway, Gerry Tricks was here, in the church (although guess what? Gerry Tricks isn't his real name!).

After Gerry had caught Charlie the woman in the pew behind started clapping and gradually everyone joined in, even Granny. Gerry's wife picked up her purple handbag and reached inside, before frowning and putting it down again. Gerry turned and raised his hand to the crowd, winked at me and gave Charlie a gentle push back towards us. And then he plugged his hearing aid back in, and in a moment he was staring into space again.

Charlie was back in the pew with us, but he wasn't happy about it.

'Take him to the special room,' whispered Mum to Dad. That sounds like a dungeon, doesn't it, but she meant the one at the back of the church. It's where they run Sunday School and have toys for babies who won't shut up.

I made my puppy dog face at Mum: you stick your bottom lip out a bit, and make your eyes look sad. It can get you anything you want, except maybe biscuits for breakfast.

'Go on, you go too,' she said, giving Dad a push.

And so we did our *excuse me, excuse me* thing, ignored Granny who was tutting quite loudly and the rest of the congregation who were staring at us as if we'd turned orange or something, and hurried to the back room.

'Phew,' said Dad as he pushed the heavy door closed behind us and looked around at all the toys. 'Safe at last. At least you can't do any damage in here.'

Dad and I watched Charlie, who was standing in the middle of the room, wrinkling his nose. 'Is for babies,' said Charlie. He picked up a cuddly monkey and sniffed it. 'Smells like cabbage.' He dropped it. He walked over and peered at one of those puzzles where each piece has a little handle and you have to fit it into a board. He picked up a fire engine piece, and jammed it in the hole for a train. It didn't fit, of course, but he didn't care. 'Is easy-peasy.' Finally he held a toy aeroplane in the air, and let go. It crashed to the ground. 'Rubbish airlane, everyone broken,' he said. He put his hands on his hips and frowned at Dad, like it was all his fault. 'I scream instead,' he said, and took a deep breath.

Dad looked behind him to check the door was closed, and kneeled down. 'Now then Pavarotti, no need for any of that. There must be something in here you can do.'

'What about the telly?' I said. 'He could watch a DVD.'

'I'm not sure that's a good idea,' said Dad, looking at the TV in the corner of the room. 'And anyway, I haven't got a Scooby Doo how to make it work.'

'I can do it,' I said. 'It's my job at Sunday School. It's easy. Any idiot can turn it on.'

'Not this idiot,' said Dad. 'And I don't think we should be watching –'

'Urr-urr-Urr-Urr-URR-URR!' Dad was interrupted by Charlie who was getting louder and louder, like a helicopter starting up its rotor blades.

'OK OK! Hurry up, Harry, this one's going to blow!' said Dad.

I ran over and turned on the DVD and the telly. It really is easy to work a TV, I don't know why grown-ups find it difficult, especially when they're the ones who invented it.

A DVD of Bible stories was in there already, and it started playing. They were cartoons, but I think they ran out of money when they made it. Noah's Ark came on. Noah looked like Chewbacca from Star Wars, the Ark had loads of holes in it and the animals looked like they'd been drawn by Charlie. With his eyes shut.

'Want somefink else,' said Charlie, and I didn't blame him. Dad was looking at his phone now so I tried to help. Bible Stories Volume 2, Volume 3, Volume 4… there wasn't much choice.

You know when your Mum says, 'Do you want to come shopping with me or stay and do your homework,' and shopping suddenly seems like fun even though you used to like it but now you find it quite boring? That's basically what happened when Charlie saw a Peppa Pig DVD stuck in between the Bible Stories.

Once upon a time Charlie *loved* Peppa. His favourite colour was pink, his favourite animal was a pig, he said Granny looked like Grampy Rabbit and he stopped talking for three days and just oinked instead. Mum got worried but Dad said you never see 10 year olds oinking like pigs, but Mum said 'I'm not waiting until he's 10 years old!' and took him to the doctors. But then on the way Charlie saw a McDonald's and started shouting 'Happy Me! Happy Me!' instead, so Mum brought him home again.

'Peppa! Peppa! Peppa! OINK!' In the room at

the back of the church, Charlie started jumping up and down in imaginary muddy puddles. Dad looked up from his phone. 'Put it on Harry, anything to keep him quiet.'

'I do it, I do it!' said Charlie, snatching the DVD out of my hands and sliding it into the DVD player – upside down.

'It not working!'

'Now you've done it,' I said, trying to find the eject button.

'I fix, is easy,' said Charlie, and he started prodding and poking his chubby fingers everywhere: pressing every switch and button he could see.

'Oi!' said Dad as the lights went off.

'I sorry,' said Charlie in the gloom. 'I fix it.'

A whirring noise started in the corner of the room, like an aeroplane. Dad flicked on the light switch, and then turned off the old fan heater that was starting to make a funny smell.

'Ah, got it!' I said as the DVD ejected and I turned it over.

'Nice one,' said Dad, returning to his phone.

The boring titles started scrolling up the screen while Charlie started to make himself comfy. First, he pushed the door completely closed, turned the massive key and pushed it into his trousers.

'Dad!' I said, but he waved me away without even looking up.

Then, he piled all the cushions and blankets in front of the telly. Then he looked around.

In the corner was a little table covered in a red chequered table cloth, with a picture of Jesus on it.

Very carefully, he lifted the picture onto the floor. 'Sorry, cheeses,' he said seriously. (He always calls Jesus that.) 'I need your carpet.' And he pulled the tablecloth off, and added it to his pile.

'Take off your jumper Daddy,' he said, standing in front of him. And Dad, without even taking his eyes off his phone, did as he was told. You can get anything from a grown-up when they're on their phone – I once got three packets of crisps.

Charlie trotted over to me. 'Take off your towsers, Harry.'

'No way,' I replied. 'Take your own off.'

'OK.' So he did. Once he had yanked his trousers over his bulging nappy pants and tugged off his red shoes he threw them on the pile and then threw himself on top, before squiggling, squirming and rearranging until he'd made himself a warm cocoon in front of the telly.

And when I say 'in front of the telly' I'm not joking: his nose was now nearly touching the screen, and he made gentle little piggy noises as he waited for the first Peppa episode to start, like a hungry pig snuffling for acorns.

I pointed the remote and selected *The biggest muddy puddle in the world*, which is Charlie's favourite. He squealed with excitement, but it didn't last long – there was no sound.

'There's no sound,' he said.

'There's no sound,' said Dad, looking up.

'I *know* there's no sound,' I said, 'I'm not a doofus. I'm turning it up.'

Except there wasn't a volume on the DVD remote, and I couldn't see a remote for the telly, and I was pretty certain it wasn't stuck up Granny's bottom this time. With Charlie making sad pig noises I reached under the telly and found the secret volume buttons they always hide there. Sure enough, the green volume bars started to march up the screen... 2, 3, 4, 5, but still no sound. No music, no splashing, and no snorting unless you counted the ones coming from the little animal in front of the telly. Why is everything always so complicated?

Outside we could hear singing: yet another hymn. It sounded dreadful: a right old dog's dinner, as Dad loves saying.

'It's not working,' I said to Dad.

'Sure it is. Just turn it right up, it's probably just set to quiet because it's a church,' replied Dad.

Now in our house we have a volume rule. We're not allowed to turn it up past number 10, even though it goes right up to number 27 (I found out one day, and almost made myself cry it was so loud). I can usually sneak it up to 12 or 13 without Mum or Dad noticing. But with Dad watching, I pressed, and I pressed, and I pressed, way on past 10, up to 15... I could just about hear Daddy Pig talking now, but it was really faint. Dad pointed up, to the ceiling, so I kept on going.

By now the noise from outside was awful, too: a big jumble of notes and voices, as if nobody knew what they were singing. They should have practised more.

The 'up' button stopped working at 30, with green volume bars right up to the top of the screen.

I could hear Peppa talking to George quite well now, but this telly was still rubbish, and Charlie was still grumbling (like a pig).

Just as Grandpa Pig was arriving in his boat, the door handle rattled, and someone started thumping.

'Let me in, for goodness sake!' came a voice outside the door.

Charlie looked alarmed. 'Is it cheeses?'

Dad looked a little surprised, too, and sprang up to open the door. 'It's locked!' he said.

'Open the door, man!' came the voice. 'You're making a mockery of our service!' The thumps continued.

Now Dad looked really worried. 'Where's the key, kids? And what on earth is the old fella talking about?'

'Charlie has the key,' I said. 'In his pocket.'

Charlie stood up and grabbed a handful of chubby white thigh with each fist. 'Look! I not got pockets! I got no towsers on!'

'TURN OFF THAT DAMN TELEVISION!' said the man outside.

'Daddy! He say a rude word! In church!' shouted Charlie, who had stopped grumbling and was now very excited.

'Why does he want the telly off?' I asked, trying to find the off switch. It wasn't in the same place as the volume control, how stupid is that.

'How should I know?' said Dad. 'And where have Charlie's flippin trousers gone?'

'IS ANOTHER RUDE WORD!' said Charlie, who looked like all his Christmases had come at once, as Mum would say. Dad, meanwhile, was too busy flapping about, throwing cushions everywhere, looking for the key.

Clang! Dad had thrown Charlie's trousers up in the air along with a cushion, and the huge metal key dropped out onto the floor. Dad snatched it up, ran across and jiggled it into the heavy wooden door before flinging it open.

The man at the door was the same one who did the reading earlier. He'd been thumping away on the door, but looking back down the church. So when Dad opened the door it caught him completely by surprise. And so his next thump whooshed through the air… and landed right onto Dad's nose.

'Aaargh!' shouted Dad.

'Let me through!' yelled the man, pushing past.

'Are you OK?' I asked.

'IS NAUGHTY!' shouted Charlie.

'Muddy puddles!' shouted Peppa.

Hang on. Who asked Peppa to say anything? And why could I suddenly hear the theme tune, 40 times louder than our telly at home?

The man strode over to the wall and flicked a switch by the plug labelled 'Church Sound System'. Suddenly the Peppa music was coming from the telly, until he switched that off at the wall too. The telly went blank, and there was silence.

I walked over and took Dad's hand, the one that wasn't rubbing his nose. Charlie took my other hand and together we walked past thumping man, who was red in the face and breathing very heavily, out into the church.

You know what it's like when you go into somewhere really big, and it's completely empty? You get that soft silence, when all you can hear is your own breathing. Well it was like that, except a bit different because about 500 people had all twisted right round in their seats and were staring at us. Actually it was 499, because I noticed that Gerry Tricks was still facing the front. Maybe that giant hearing aid of his didn't work very well.

Nobody said a word, and we stood there for a moment.

The soft thud of a closing door broke the silence, and through a glass panel we could see Mum helping Granny out through the main exit. Mum took one look over her shoulder, before hurrying on.

'Trousers,' hissed Dad.

'What?' I said.

'Trousers! Get Charlie's trousers!'

Oh yes. I broke out of the Dad-Charlie sandwich and grabbed them from the little room.

'Just smile and wave,' whispered Dad as we walked across the church, followed by 998 eyes.

The vicar, now back at the front, held up her hand. 'BYE!' shouted Charlie, waving back, and then at the rest of the congregation. 'Happy Kissmas!' And with one final push of the big door, we were free.

You'll never guess who visited us at Granny's house later that day. It wasn't thumping man: that would have been a bit awkward, especially because Dad had to sit with a bag of peas on his face for most of the day. And it wasn't the vicar, although we heard later that she thought it was the best Easter service she'd ever given.

Nope, it was Gerry Tricks and his wife, who I'll have to call Mrs Tricks because I don't know her real name and I never will because she stood behind him on the step, looking shy. Gerry had brought back all the stuff we'd left in the pew.

'That's so kind,' said Mum as he handed it over. Mum spoke really loudly, about as loudly as you can without actually shouting.

'No problem, I didn't want to let my little mate down,' said Gerry in his booming voice, ruffling Charlie's hair.

'How's the beak doing?' he asked Dad. 'Stanley gave you a right belter, I heard.'

'It's a dit detter dow, dank you,' said Dad through his peas.

'Sorry you missed all the fun, Francesca,' he said to Granny, who was limping downstairs. It took me a minute to work out he meant Granny. I'm not even sure I knew her name before.

'MY MOTHER HAD A FUNNY TURN,' said-shouted Mum.

Charlie made a silly face and spun around. 'I can do funny turns too,' he said.

Granny harrumphed.

'You're quite the ballroom dancer, aren't you, chubby legs?' said Gerry. (Charlie still hadn't got his trousers back on.)

'IT'S GOOD TO SEE YOU UP AND ABOUT, CHARLES,' yelled Mum. (So that was his real name. I think I'll stick with Gerry.) 'ARE YOU MUCH BETTER?'

'Yep, I'm right as rain now. And my hearing's pretty good, too,' he said, grinning.

'Oh, I'm sorry,' said Mum in a normal voice. She blushed. 'I thought...?" She looked at the side of Gerry's head. His hearing aid was gone.

'Oh that?' said Gerry. He laughed. 'You must be the only one who doesn't know.'

Granny made a harrumphing sound, but it didn't look like she was going to have another funny turn. She crossed her arms.

Mrs Tricks leaned forward, as if she wanted to share a secret with us. 'He listens to the racing,' she said in a mousy voice. 'Or cricket. Or football.'

'Anything except that dreary old vicar,' said Gerry.

Granny slammed the door to the kitchen.

'I don't think Francesca approves,' said Gerry.

'It's the only way I can get him to come,' squeaked Mrs Tricks, smiling. 'Still, I think he missed the best bit of the service today.'

Mum shook her head, and put her arms around me and Charlie. Dad didn't have any hands free – it was quite a big bag of peas.

After a bit more chit-chat, they were off.

'Close the door, Harry,' said Mum, but just before the lock clicked I heard that mouse voice again. 'Ooh, children! You forgot something else!'

I opened the door. Gerry was miles away already, but Mrs Tricks was standing by the gate with her big purple handbag. 'Come here, both of you!'

I looked at Charlie, and Charlie looked at me. We approached her carefully: what if she had a bomb in that bag? Or a snake?

She reached in and rummaged around. There was a rustling sound. 'Something to keep you both going,' she said, pulling out a huge bag of toffees.

'One's never enough, is it? I always carry spares, just in case,' she squeaked, before handing them over and scuttling off up the road after Gerry.

Country Fair

'I want my party bag.'

That was Charlie, who'd been asking for it since we left home about thirty thousand hours ago.

'That's not a good idea,' said Dad. 'Remember what happened with the bubbles. Let's wait until we get out of the car.'

'But it's taking for *ages!*' said Charlie.

Charlie was right: this was the longest car journey in the world. (Dad was right, too: Charlie shouldn't open party bags in the car, not after last time. You had to admit, though, it had been a good idea, holding his bubble wand out of the car window. We both thought that hundreds of bubbles would stream down the road after our car and it would look really cool. It didn't happen. The wind ripped the wand straight out of his hand

and it landed on the windscreen of a police car behind us. Whoops.)

As Charlie complained to Dad our car inched forwards towards a gate. A man in a bright orange vest was standing guard under a huge 'Country Show' banner, taking money from each car.

'Maybe we could just have one thing from our party bags,' I said. 'Just to keep us going.'

Mum sighed, reached down to her feet and pulled out the stripy paper bags. 'There's an aeroplane, and a balloon, and a book, and a lolly. No bubble mixture, thank goodness. Which do you want, as if I have to ask?'

'Lolly! Lolly!' Charlie and I shouted.

'If you get your sticky fingers on my seats,' said Dad, 'you'll be cleaning this car yourself and then I'll make you clean my trousers too and – oh, hello.' Dad had reached the front of the queue. 'Two adults, two kids, please.'

'Twenty pounds please fella,' chirped the man in the orange jacket.

Dad coughed, and humphed. Mum handed him the money. As we drove off, Dad carried on humphing. 'Twenty quid! This better be good. We only want to come for the day, not buy the farm.'

'Oh cheer up,' said Mum, unwrapping Charlie's lolly and handing it back. 'We'll have a great day out, I'm sure. Or we will as soon as we finally get out of this thing.'

By now we were bumping across the grass towards a row of parked cars. From there people were carrying boxes, bags and even fold-up chairs towards the next field, which was crowded with marquees and stalls.

'Hmm,' said Dad. 'Well if it's just a bunch of farmers showing off about the size of their bullocks, I'll be asking for my money back.'

'Ignore him,' said Mum. 'He's just being a miserable old goat.'

'Maybe there'll be a competition for the 'Most Miserable Old Goat,' I said.

'Daddy not a goat,' said Charlie, who was poking at his lolly.

'Thank you, Charlie,' said Dad, looking for a space.

'He a piggy-wig.'

'Charming child. Now if that car in front would just move forward a bit –'

Dad's grumbling and moaning was drowned out by an ear-piercing whistle.

'Aaargh!' we all said, and pressed our hands against our ears.

'Stop it Charlie!' yelled Mum.

Charlie grinned. 'Is a storeberry toot sweet!' he said. 'Harry, you got a toot sweet?'

I unwrapped mine: he was right. You know what a toot sweet is, don't you? You will if you've ever watched *Chitty Chitty Bang Bang*. It's my Granny's favourite film, and Charlie's too. There's this mad inventor who invents a lolly that's also a whistle, but it makes all the dogs go crazy.

I gave mine a little blow. It was just like Charlie's, but orange flavoured and the sound was a bit lower. There was a bit at the bottom you could push in to change the note, too. I looked at Charlie and mouthed 'One, two, three…'

'Weee-oooo-weee-ooo!'

It sounded like a train whistle.

'ENOUGH!' Dad stopped the car. 'I'd pay forty quid just to get away from you noisy lot.'

''Call it fifty and you've got a deal,' said Mum. 'Come on, let's see what this fair has to offer.'

Quite a lot, it seemed. Stalls were selling food, funny owls made out of tin cans, horse riding equipment, spare parts for tractors, wellies, coloured boomerangs and more. It was like someone had collected all the weird things in the world and decided to sell them in a field in the middle of nowhere.

Charlie, with his whistle lolly hanging around his neck, held my hand and sang as we walked along.

Tinkle Tinkle, haf you any wool,
Yes sir yes sir, see how dey run,
One for the donkey, on a rusty road
One for the little boy, wiv the shiny nose.

'That's very good,' I said. I didn't mean it, but sometimes you're supposed to say nice things; they're like a special kind of lie that's OK.

'Is my happy song,' said Charlie. 'You want it again?'

'Err, maybe later,' I said. And by later, I meant never.

'Hey, look at all these!'

We'd left the stalls behind now and we were in

the next field, full of fairground rides. I could see dodgems, waltzers, those stalls where you can win a cuddly toy if you can throw a ball in the bucket but you never can because they always bounce out, and some of those Chair-o-Planes where you sit in a chair on chains, and it whizzes round high in the air. No chance of me going on that – I get a funny tummy at the top of the climbing frame.

The noise was incredible: shrieking, clanking and hooting from the rides, and screams from the people on them. The dodgems were nearest, but they looked fast and sounded dangerous – angry electricity sparked from the ceiling. So I pushed Mum and Dad forward to the carousel. Around and around it whizzed, with horses bobbing up and down, and the organ blaring out a tune that was even worse than Charlie's song.

'Can we? Can we?' I asked.

Mum smiled. 'Let's do it.'

Charlie's eyes lit up. 'Yay! I good at riding horses!'

'Really?' said Dad. 'How much is it?'

'Are you going to complain about money *all* day?' said Mum. 'Don't worry kids, I'll get this one.'

So we waited until the carousel slowed to a halt and everyone got off, and then we climbed on board. Charlie got into a rocket, but then we told him it didn't go up and down so he climbed up in front of Mum on horse number 8, *Buster*. I was alongside on horse 3, *Tricksy*, and Dad was behind on 32, *Mr Plod*.

The man came round to collect the money. But the next thing I knew, Mum was lifting Charlie off the horse, and holding out her hand for me to do the same!

'You've got a nerve. That's daylight robbery!' she said over her shoulder to the man with the money bag. He shrugged, and held out his hand to Dad. He jabbed his finger a bit towards Mum to show he was with her, even if he didn't want to be, and jumped down off Mr Plod.

'Twenty pounds!' said Mum as she pulled us away, ignoring Charlie's screams. Mum was very unhappy, and I wasn't crazy about it either. 'For about five minutes! They must think we were born yesterday.' She blew out and her cheeks wobbled, just like a hot horse. Tricksy, probably, if he was a real horse. 'And you can zip it too, Mr I-Told-You-So,' she said to Dad.

'I'm saying nothing,' said Dad, smiling.

This was turning out to be a rubbish Country Fair. We needed a diversion. 'What's that?' I said.

The next stall had caught my attention because there were so many people crowded around, and I liked the crazy sign: *Barrie's Bucking Bronco*. Above the heads of the crowd we could just see a woman with her hand in the air. She was spinning around, her hair flying out in every direction, yelling 'Yee-ha!' at the top of her voice, like a cowboy. Or a cowgirl. And then suddenly she disappeared, a hooter sounded and the crowd whooped and cheered.

Charlie and I used our super skills to squeeze through to the barrier. In the middle of a circle was a mechanical bull, or more like three quarters of a bull because it didn't have a head, and it had a big handle sticking out of its back.

A huge man with a bushy beard and flowery shorts was trying to get on. He hauled on the handle and tried to throw his giant leg over the bull's back. But he didn't quite make it, and fell off onto an inflatable mattress. Everyone nudged each other and laughed.

'You alright Terry?' shouted a woman with

frizzy hair and a crazy skirt that matched Terry's shorts. She bounced out to the middle and pushed her hand into Terry's flabby bottom as he tried to get up again.

Dad and Mum joined us at the barrier.

'Look, clowns!' Charlie said to Dad, pointing to the man and the woman.

'Charlie! Keep your voice down!' said Mum.

'He's right, though,' said Dad. 'They haven't even started the bronco up yet and he's falling off.'

'What's a bonko?' said Charlie.

'You'll see, sweetheart.' Dad tutted. 'That man really hasn't got a clue.'

'Dad's an expert,' said Mum, putting her arm around his shoulder. 'He's told me many, many times how he won a bronco challenge at college, and even got a kiss from a pretty girl.'

'Was it you?' I asked.

'No! It wasn't! Can you believe it?' said Mum.

'I bet she wasn't as pretty as you,' I said.

'Thank you, lovely daughter,' said Mum, smiling.

'I bet she looked like Mr Plod.'

'Oi!' said Dad, giving me a kick up the bum. 'I can't help it if I'm drop-dead gorgeous,' said Dad.

'And you're right, I'm brilliant at the bronco.'

Mum raised her eyebrows.

'I am. It's because I grew up on the Texas plains, wrangling cattle. Real broncos... well, they're almost like friends to someone like me,' said Dad, looking up and stroking his chin.

'He's talking out of his bottom again, kids,' said Mum.

'Ah, those were the days,' said Dad. 'Just me and my trusty horse.'

'What your horse called, Daddy?' asked Charlie.

'Dog Food Dolly,' said Dad. 'Lovely filly, she was. We'd set out with a flask full of orange squash and some digestives and spend weeks under that big Texan sky... '

'What's Dad on about?' I asked.

'It beats me,' said Mum. 'Are you OK?' she asked. 'Do you need a lie down?'

'These things,' said Dad, waving his arm at the bronco... 'they're OK for the kids, I suppose.' I think he thought he was being mysterious, but he just looked a bit like a dingbat.

Only Charlie looked impressed. Mum and I knew that Dad grew up in a semi-detached house in Birmingham, he's never been to Texas, can't ride a horse and certainly hasn't wangled any cattle, whatever that means.

We turned back to the action. Back in the ring, Terry in the flowery shorts wasn't happy. Probably because his girlfriend had her hand up his bottom.

'Gerroff me Tina!' he grunted. He was stuck now, his top half flopped over the saddle and his bottom half on Tina's head, like a fat, flowery hat. 'I can do it… I can do it… I can –'

He slid off and landed in a heap on top of poor Tina.

The hooter sounded, and the crowd whistled and laughed while a red-faced Terry and Tina crawled off the mattress.

'That's definitely a record!' said a small, ratty-faced man with a microphone. I guessed that was Barrie, and this was his Bucking Bronco. 'So who's next? Come along, who'll be our next have-a-go hero?'

A loud, fruity whistle rang out. Charlie, who was stood up on the railings, was punching his hand in the air. He's only just learned to do this at preschool, and is very proud. Not the whistle bit, I mean, the hand-up bit. He spat out his toot sweet and yelled. 'Me, me, me!'

'Not you, sunshine,' said Barrie, pointing to a sign behind him. 'Thirteen years or older.'

'But you said, you said, you said, dey is just for kids!' said Charlie to Dad, his face creasing up.

'He's right,' said Mum. 'You did say that.'

'Sorry, Charlie, I was just being daft,' admitted Dad, ruffling Charlie's hair. Charlie stuck out his bottom lip in disgust.

'Brilliant,' announced Barrie. 'We have a volunteer!' We all looked around to see who it would be.

'Come along then, sir, show your boys what you're made of!' He seemed to be looking directly at Dad and waving his hand. And then I realised why: Mum was behind him, pointing her finger at Dad's head with a big grin on her face.

I was pretty annoyed about Barrie calling me a boy. He was obviously an idiot.

Dad shook his head. 'No way.'

'Go on, hot shot,' said Mum. 'Imagine you're back in Texas.'

'Cah-mon! Cah-mon! Cah-mon!' The crowd started chanting. I started chanting. Even Charlie started chanting.

Dad really didn't have any choice. Shaking his head and waving his fist at Mum, he climbed over the railings and into the ring.

With a reluctant nod to the crowd, Dad bounced to the centre of the circle and grabbed hold of the bull's handle. Trying to look as sporty as possible, he jumped up into the saddle. In fact he sprang so far he almost fell off on the other side. Mum giggled.

'Looks like we have ourselves a cool customer,' said Barrie to the audience before putting down his microphone. With a couple of steps he was by Dad's side, and they talked for a minute. Dad started waving his arms and looking like he'd got the hump, as Mum would say. But eventually he reached into his tight trouser pockets for a £10 note and handed it over to Barrie. He pulled a face at Mum.

Barrie was back on the mic. 'Let's hope he can hold on to Bully as tightly as he holds on to his money, eh boys and girls?' Everyone laughed and Dad went red. 'Right, let's give him a whirl!'

Barrie gave a thumbs up to a girl chewing gum in a cubicle behind him, and loud music blared out of the speakers. As the bull started to revolve slowly, Dad grinned nervously. He put his hand in the air for a moment and tried to wave it like the girl had done, but he quickly put it down again so he could hold on with two hands.

'Is easy!' said Charlie. 'Daddy, is easy!' he shouted out. Daddy didn't hear; he was too busy looking at his hands, as if that would help him hold on.

Bully lurched forward and Dad followed, onto his tummy. Bully jerked backwards, and so did Dad; I reckon only the handle stopped him being catapulted right back to the car park.

'He looks a bit scared,' I said.

'He's petrified,' said Mum. 'It's brilliant.'

Suddenly, with a whir and a hiss, Bully sprang into life. Well not really, that would be quite weird, but it started jumping and bumping all over the place. But Dad didn't give up: he held onto that handle like it was his last fruity chew. He flopped this way and that way like Woody from *Toy Story*. The crowd cheered when it looked like he was going to fall off, and groaned when he recovered.

'Why doesn't he just give up?' I asked Mum.

'I've no idea,' she said. 'Maybe he really thinks he's John Wayne.'

I had no idea who John Wayne was, and there was no time to ask. At that moment Bully did a particularly vicious back-forwards flip. The bottom end of Dad, the bit not holding on, went flying up into the air. Dad's skinny legs flew in different directions before they realised they were attached to the other bit of him and couldn't go flying off wherever they wanted, and he landed back in the saddle with a massive thump.

Everyone winced, and Dad went a bit red. He even took one hand off his saddle to rub his bum.

But Bully didn't rest for long and soon Dad was flying again. Suddenly the crowd wasn't cheering, or booing, but laughing. One girl actually sprayed out her mouthful of fizzy drink. And as Dad span round we found out why.

Dad wasn't holding his bum because it was sore. He was trying to cover up a massive rip in his skinny brown trousers, a ragged hole that went right from his belt down to the bottom of his bottom. And through this huge, flapping tear we could see Dad's pink pants.

I should probably explain that these pants weren't pink when Dad bought them. They were white. But *someone* poked a pink felt tip into the washing machine, and nobody noticed. So his pants went in the colour of snow and came out the colour of a pretty sunset.

Dad hadn't been very pleased. 'Charlie!' he'd shouted. (I think he was just guessing who the Phantom Pink Pen Pusher was, but it was a very good guess.) 'If I'd wanted Barbie pants I'd have bought them from the shop!'

I laughed. Charlie laughed. Mum laughed a lot. And even Dad laughed a little in the end, even though he said he'd never wear them again, or maybe just on days when he'd run out of clean ones.

This was obviously one of those days. Maybe it was the embarrassment, maybe it was Bully's acrobatics, but Dad couldn't take it any longer. He zinged off onto the mattress, and rolled across to Mum like a caterpillar.

'Let's give him a big hand!' said Barrie. 'Bet you didn't think you'd end up showing everyone your wife's pants, did you?'

Dad was perched on top of the barrier, trying to climb back over without anyone seeing. 'What?' he spluttered, turning even redder. 'They're not my wife's pants! They're mine!' he shouted, to even more laughter.

'Yes yes, we believe you,' said Barrie, winking at the audience. '*Of course* those nice tight pink pants are yours. *Of course* they are. And anyway, whatever you wear under those tight trousers, well that's your business eh? Right, on with the show! Who's next?'

Mum was laughing so much she could hardly help Dad off the barrier, and when he did reach the ground he crouched down so nobody could see his pants, and then hopped away, like a frog. 'Come on!' he said, waving us on. 'I need to get away from here!'

Charlie crouched down too and hopped along behind him, and Mum and I followed. The crowd opened up to let us through, and I noticed that some people were filming him on their phones. Charlie noticed too, and gave them a wave as we went past.

'We frogs!' he said happily, as if it was the most natural thing in the world to hop through a Country Fair behind your dad in his pants.

'What are we going to do?' said Dad, still crouching.

We were hiding behind a hot dog stall; Mum had shooed away the small bunch of children that had followed us from the scene of his disaster.

'What are *we* going to do? Who's this *we* you're talking about?' said Mum, still laughing. 'I'm doing just fine. Here, Harry, you're better at this than I am. You know what to do.'

Mum handed me her phone; the camera was already on. 'No problem, Mum.'

I crouched down low behind Dad, so I could get a good pic. He realised what I was doing just as I took the picture, looking over his shoulder with a grumpy face.

'Oi!' he said. 'You'd better not put that on –'

'– Instagram? Too late, I already did,' I said, sharing it using Mum's account and tagging it #pinkpants.

'Pinky pants, stinky pants, pinky pants, stinky pants!' said Charlie, hopping up behind Dad and waving his hand in front of his nose.

'You lot are hilarious,' said Dad, not sounding amused. 'I can't go round like this!'

'We could go home?' I said.

'We can't go home now,' said Mum. 'I'm just starting to have fun. And besides, we paid through the nose to get in here and it's not even lunchtime!'

'There's only one thing for it,' said Dad. 'You'll just have to buy me some trousers.'

'No problem,' said Mum sarcastically. 'I'll just pop into the nearest department store and –oh, silly me. THERE AREN'T ANY SHOPS. You'll just have to wear your pants. They look a bit like shorts anyway. Pink shorts.'

'No they don't,' I said. 'Not at all. If you bought me shorts like that I'd go back to the shop and ask for your money back.'

Dad paused for a moment, trying to understand me. 'Thanks for the support Harry. I think.' He shifted from one buttock to another to stop some spiky hay from going up his bottom.

'Besides,' I said, there *is* a trouser shop.'

'Where?'

'Back where we came in. Lots of colours. I noticed it had a funny name.'

'Go on… ' said Dad. 'Why do I feel nervous?'

'It was called *A Juicy Pair*.'

Mum collapsed into giggles.

'I love juicy pears!' said Charlie. 'Can we get one? Can we?'

'No way. No way. You are not buying me some new strides from a shop called *Juicy Pears*.'

'I'm not sure you've got much option, have you?' said Mum through her tears. 'You just stay here with your froggy mate and Harry and I will choose you a nice, juicy pair.'

'Mum, they're all the same!' I said. 'I mean, they're different colours, but they're all weird!'

The stall was about the size of our living room. Rows of trousers sparkled and shimmered, and at the back a lanky man with a tight white shirt and a fabulous twirly moustache leaned on the counter.

'Not weird,' said Mum, glancing at the man, 'just... '

'Swell?' drawled the man. 'Dazzling? Groovy? Far out? Any of those do the trick, princess?' He grinned a yellow-toothed grin. I thought he might be calling *me* a princess – I hate that – but actually he was looking at Mum. I shuddered.

'I'm not sure they're quite right. Thank you!' said Mum. She grabbed my hand. 'We'll go somewhere else,' she said under her breath.

'Nowhere else to go,' called out the man, who obviously had hearing like a bat. 'They didn't even want me here, selling my awesome loons, but I came anyway.'

'What are loons?' I whispered.

'Loon pants,' said the man. I should have guessed he'd hear me. I reckon he could hear a cow do a silent trump in the next field. 'Bell bottoms. They're the only leg curtains a man should own.'

Just as I was scratching my head at the idea of anyone calling trousers 'leg curtains', there was a loud thump. The man had swung his bright orange, sequinned leg up onto the counter, and left it there for us to inspect. His trouser leg was tight at the top – very tight indeed – and then it ballooned out below the knee. Like a bell, I suppose, or a jazzy parachute. A small foot in a brown boot stuck out from the pile of orange material.

'Wow.' I said.

'Wow indeed,' said Mum.

'We've got to get Dad *something*,' I said. 'He can't jump around like a frog all day.'

Mum looked at the man's trousers. 'But... I mean really Harry... How much are they, out of interest?'

'Normally forty. But today, for you only, it's a special show price – any pair, twenty pounds.' Did everything at this show cost twenty pounds?

The man still had his tangerine leg stuck up on the counter. As we watched he opened his mouth slightly and out slithered a long, lizardy tongue. This pink thing was incredible: it waved this way and that, as if it was looking for its prey. And then it curved upwards and hooked in the end of the man's long moustache before dragging it back into its dark mouth cave. Slowly, without ever taking his eyes off Mum, the man started to chew.

'I don't know,' she said, turning to avoid his gaze. 'I suppose it would solve a problem.'

'And look, we can get him a nice colour.'

We could get him any colour we wanted, it seemed; the whole rainbow was here.

'I think just something plain, like black or dark blue,' said Mum. 'He's going to go mad enough as it is.'

'Nothing plain in my den,' called out the man. This was getting ridiculous: Mum had barely spoken in more than a whisper, and I could hardly hear her above the music and shouts from the fair.

He was right, though; every pair was a zinger. Peppa Pig pink? Banana yellow? Grass green? Swimming pool blue?

'These are probably the least offensive, and they're in his size,' said Mum, looking back at the man. He raised an eyebrow and stroked his thigh.

She pulled out a heavily patterned, deep purple pair, the kind of colour a queen would wear (although maybe not the same style). As she held them up the bell bottoms flapped gently and the sequins sparkled like sunlight on rippled water.

'They're awesome,' I said. 'He'll love them.'

Mum hesitated, and then walked over and placed them on the counter. They draped over the man's right leg, which was still on the counter: purple and orange does *not* go together.

Without moving his leg, he bundled Dad's new trousers into a carrier bag.

He opened his mouth and the end of his moustache coiled back into position, damp with spit. 'Fifteen pounds,' he said, looking directly at Mum.

'You said twenty?'

'Fifteen. Show special, for my very best customers.'

Mum handed over a note. 'I'll give you twenty. Thank you very much, goodbye!'

She grabbed the carrier bag and pulled, except she was in such a hurry she grabbed his orange trouser leg too. She yanked and the man's leg rotated towards her, like a minute hand on a crazy clock. He looked at Mum the way you'd look at a nice cream cake, his tongue popping out again. With a little yelp, Mum grabbed me and we were off.

'WHAT a weirdo,' said Mum as left.

'Tell your Dad she couldn't keep her hands off me!' the man called after us as we hurried away. 'Catch you on the flip side!'

'Mum?'

'I've no idea what it means,' Mum said. 'Don't

92

look back, Harry, in case he's doing something funny with his leg again.'

How much do you think Dad liked his new trousers? If you guessed 'as much as I like times tables,' you're right.

'You're having a laugh,' he said. 'What have I done to deserve those?'

'I knew you'd appreciate them,' said Mum. 'Harry and I chose them very carefully. You owe me twenty pounds.'

'They were going to be fifteen,' I added, 'but Mum wanted to pay twenty.'

Dad frowned.

'Don't ask,' said Mum. 'Just put 'em on.'

As the hot dog man looked on and laughed, Dad tried to wiggle into them. They were so tight he had to lie on his back and wriggle them up over his hips.

'Dey upside down you silly billy!' said Charlie, and I knew why he said it: they looked bigger at the bottom than at the top.

Mum helped him to his feet.

'You look… hot,' said Mum.

'Oh?'

'Sweaty.'

'I think I look pretty foxy,' said Dad, taking a few practice paces up and down, swinging his hips and singing. '*You can tell by the way I use my walk I'm a woman's man.*'

'I can tell by the way you walk you need a poo,' I said.

The hot dog man whistled. 'So fabulous, dahling!'

Dad gave him a wave like he was on the catwalk, and we rejoined the crowds.

We wandered on past the fairground rides and soon we were in Dad's idea of a nightmare: animals being led around a pen while people leaned on the railings and pointed at them.

As we arrived, it was the cows' turn. These huge, muscly beasts were being pulled along by skinny boys and girls; they looked like they could be gulped up at any moment. Each cow was guided past three men in white coats who stood with clipboards, talking quietly to each other before walking around each animal and occasionally giving them a bit of a squeeze. It was all very odd.

The cows were then parked up in a row, each with their own driver.

'What dey doing?' asked Charlie.

'They're playing cow dominoes,' said Dad. 'In a minute they'll push the end one over, and then they'll all fall down.'

Charlie looked at Dad. 'You silly.'

'You're right, Charlie, he is,' said Mum. 'It's a competition, to see which cow is the… umm… '

'Meatiest?' I said.

'Milkiest?' said Dad.

'Fattest?' said Charlie.

'You're nearest, Charlie,' said Mum. 'They're trying to find out which one is the 'Best in Show.'

The tallest of the three men walked across and stood in front of a cow, which looked just like the other ones as far as I could see, and held up one finger. The crowd cheered, a bit.

'I want to ride the brown one,' said Charlie.

Mum shook her head. 'You can't ride cows.'

'Oh! but Daddy did a ride on a bull. Is not fair.' Charlie pushed out his bottom lip.

An old man next to us smiled.

'*And* we not ride the roundy-roundy horses,' Charlie continued.

By now the cows were being led away, and men were throwing bales of hay around and moving barriers.

'What dey doing?' said Charlie again.

'No idea,' said Dad.

The old man leaned down to speak to Charlie. He had wiry grey whiskers growing from all kinds of odd places like his nose and his ear lobes. Charlie reached out his thumb and finger and gave a nose hair a tug.

The old man's eyes watered a bit, but he didn't seem to mind.

'They're getting ready for the sheepdog trials, little one,' he said. 'They're going to have a competition, see which dog is the best at driving the sheep into the pen.'

'Driving sheep?' said Charlie. 'Into a pen?' He laughed. 'Mummy say Daddy drive like a idiot. He never drive into a pen though.'

The old man took off his cap, scratched his balding head, and smiled. 'No, I don't suppose he does. I'm Harry, by the way.' He held out his hand, and held it there while Charlie turned it over to see what was on the other side.

'I'm Harry too,' I said. 'He's Charlie.'

'A pleasure to meet you,' said Harry, winking up at Mum and Dad.

'How will the dog know what to do?' I asked.

'It's all very mysterious,' said Harry. (I'll call him Harry the Big from now on, so you don't get confused.) 'Secrets of a generation. Whistles, shouts, and a bit of farmer magic. You'll see. Keep your eye on the young'un with the red cap, he's got what it takes. He'll lick those pesky sheep into shape.'

'He lick the sheep? What shape?' asked Charlie.

'You're quite the literal one, aren't you?' said Harry the Big. 'I just mean those sheep will fall over themselves to jump into that pen.'

Charlie looked up at Mum. 'He means the man with the red cap will win.'

With a metallic clank, one of the stewards opened a corner gate. Bleating and bumping into each other, a small flock of brown sheep with white heads bumbled into the arena.

'Can we ride the sheep?' said Charlie to Harry the Big. 'They look very comfy.'

'I'm afraid not,' he said. 'You'd think so, wouldn't you? Especially for a little nipper like you. But they'd be useless, they don't go in a straight line for more than about ten feet. You'd likely go round in circles.'

'I can't ride anyfink!' protested Charlie. 'Dis fair is rubbish.'

'Charlie!' scolded Mum. 'We paid an arm and a leg to get in, and we're going to enjoy ourselves whether you like it or not.'

'Ah, sorry about that,' said our new neighbour.

'Hardly your fault,' said Dad. 'Probably a greedy landowner, looking to make a quick buck.'

'Or it could be a rotten council official, making him pay for the police and the stewards and the road closures, all because he wants the Country Fair moved to his land, even though it's been here for 120 years. The same fella who won't let the Scouts camp in his field any more, wears a silly waistcoat and gets 1st prize for his cattle from his son-in-law,' sighed the man. He suddenly looked about 120 years old himself, and I thought he was about to cry.

Mum and Dad looked at him.

'Do you live round here?' asked Mum.

'Aye. You could say that,' he said. 'Oh yes, you could definitely say that.'

'Alex!' The old man had raised his hands to his mouth and was shouting across to a younger man in a red cap. 'Don't you go messin' up, d'ya hear? I've told this little'un you're the best thing since sliced bread! Don't let an old man down!'

'I'd best go and give him a few tips,' he said to us. 'These kids, they don't know they're born.' He smiled, and looked down at me. 'Present company excepted, of course, I'm sure you're a very smart youngster. Just like your brother, wherever he is.'

Good point. Where was he?

Mum sent me on a mission to find Charlie, but I didn't have to look far. He'd toddled up the railings to the corner near the sheep pen. The crowds were thinner here. I gave Mum a wave and climbed up next to him.

'I want ride somefink Harry.'

'I know, Charlie. We could pretend we're riding a horsey now, if you want?'

'No. Is not real. Or big. Or fun. Is just a gate.'

We watched in silence. Some sheep were huddled in a corner while others had strayed a bit further away. A couple more hadn't even left the corner pen. A red-faced man jumped down behind them and with a few claps and shouts, sent the lazy ones skittering into the big open space to join the others.

The judges from the cow competition were back, and Alex – the man with the red cap that the old man had been talking about – walked out with them to stand by a pole in the middle. He was wearing a t-shirt and jeans, and close by his side was a sleek, black dog. As they walked, Alex bent down and gave her a pat.

'Ladies and gentlemen, please welcome our first contestant, Alex Findlay and Sally the Wonderdog!'

The audience laughed and clapped politely, and then fell silent.

The sheep grazed happily, although I swear the one closest to Sally the Wonderdog was watching her out of the corner of its woolly eye.

Alex grinned. He leaned down and gave Sally a few final rubs of encouragement, and with a word in her ear sent her running up the field, right around the back of the sheep. 'Steady, steady,' he shouted in a low calming voice, and sometimes whistling. The sound was amazing: low, then high, and sometimes whizzing in between. Sally the Wonderdog ran, lay down in the grass, zigzagged back and forth, and gradually the sheep bunched together.

'What dey doing?' asked Charlie.

'I'm not sure,' I said. 'I think he has to get them through the gate.'

I was right. Sally chased them in slow motion around the field; every time one of them made a run for it, Alex would whistle and Sally would be there, scaring the sheep back to its friends. Finally the sheep decided they'd had enough and trotted through the gate, and the crowd applauded. Alex lifted his cap towards the old man in the crowd, and grinned.

'Great stuff, well done Alex, well done Sally!' We heard the announcer rustle her papers. 'So then, next to trial is our very own hardworking councillor and new sponsor of the town's hanging baskets, Sean Crooksmoor! Welcome Sean, looks like Alex has set you a tough target to beat, let's see what you and Megan can do!'

Sean Crooksmoor stomped out to the centre post. This man was the opposite of Alex Findlay. He was wearing baggy checked trousers that stopped just below his knees, funny lace-up shoes and socks that were pulled right up tight, with ribbons on. He wore a tartan hat with a feather in it, a red waistcoat which was stretched tight over his tummy, and his nose was red and bulging, too. He took no notice of his dog Megan, who followed him with her head down.

'He look rude,' said Charlie.

'I agree.'

'I think maybe he eated too many sausage rolls.'

'Maybe.'

'Or he had to sit on the naughty step for ages and now he sad.'

'Could be that, too.'

But he cheered up a bit when the crowd applauded. The trial had been reset with new sheep, and one of the judges signalled for him to start.

What a difference! Instead of low calls and gentle whistles, Sean Crooksmoor sounded like he was using a set of power tools to control

Megan. It was a non-stop barrage of noise. He yelled at the top of his voice – 'TAKE YOUR TIME! TAKE YOUR TIME!', made noises like a cat who's got stuck in a catflap, and whistled, long, harsh, high whistles.

But though it was different, you had to admit it was working. Megan dashed backwards and forwards at lightning speed, rarely still for a moment. At one point a sheep made a run for it – maybe it didn't like all the shouting - but Crooksmoor gave an ear-splitting roar at the dog who streaked across to bring the poor sheep back to the group.

The sheep were up in our corner now, furthest away from the post, the judges, and Crooksmoor. They paused for a moment, with one sheep deciding it was a good time to take a munch.

At the sound of a low whistle Megan ran round and darted at the group. Two sheep went left, four went right. Crooksmoor thundered another command, and Megan was back, but another higher whistle sent her too far, and the four sheep split into three and one. This was odd; Megan seemed be making a right muck of it.

Another strange thing, too: the whistles

sounded different. Although sound was echoing around the showground because of the speakers, this whistle was higher, and closer. Much closer.

Can you guess who it was? If you guessed Charlie, you're right. He was watching the sheep and Megan intensely with his toot sweet in his mouth, occasionally blowing it gently to send Megan off course.

'Charlie!' I said as quietly as I could. 'What are you doing?'

'I helping the doggy,' he said. 'Is fun. You try!'

I'd forgotten about my whistle, which was still hanging around my neck. Looking around nervously, I gave it the smallest puff, a toot as quiet as a trump under your duvet. Well not *your* duvet, obviously, more like a toot under my duvet.

Megan changed direction and Crooksmoor yelled again.

Charlie whistled; Megan responded.

I gave mine another blow, and she streaked back the other way.

By now, only two sheep were still friends. The other four were running all over the place, like toddlers at soft play. Crooksmoor was now waving his arms around in anger while the judges scribbled on their clipboards and shook their heads.

'Charlie, time to stop,' I said. 'If they see us with these whistles, we'll be in big trouble.'

'I eat it,' said Charlie. And with five crunchy crunches his whistle was gone.

'Come on, Charlie, let's find Mummy.'

I pushed my sticky whistle into my shirt pocket and pulled Charlie away, back into the crowds.

We went the long way round, which Charlie never likes. By the time we got back to Mum and Dad he was moaning again about having 'nuffink' to ride on, and he squeezed past Harry the Big to hug Mum's leg. The next contestant was out at the pole, yelling and whistling at his dog.

Mum raised her eyebrows at me.

'What?' I said.

'Have you two been behaving?' she said. She had one of those looks, the ones that means she already thinks she knows what has happened.

'Of course,' I said, pulling my lolly out of my pocket. It was covered in fluff. I put it in my mouth, to stop me having to speak.

Harry the Big looked down and noticed us. 'Ah, you've found him, then! You've missed all the action!' he said to Charlie.

'It almost got interesting for a moment,' said Dad. 'The hot favourite fell to pieces when his dog went a bit loopy. Look, there he is. Still livid by the looks of it.'

Dad pointed; Crooksmoor was standing outside the window of a caravan signposted JUDGES at the end of the field. His waistcoat flapped as he shouted at a poor woman trapped inside.

'It couldn't have happened to a nicer chap,' said Harry the Big. As he spoke, Alex – the man with the red cap – walked up and put his arm around Harry the Big's shoulders. Sally the Wonderdog sat on Harry's feet.

'Well done, son,' said Harry. 'You did pretty well. Almost as good as your old man.'

Alex punched him on the shoulder. At that moment a big cheer rose from the crowd, and people clapped.

Alex looked across to the man walking back from the pole with his dog and a big grin. 'I'm not sure we've done enough to win, but at least it won't be a shoe-in for Mr Angry,' said Alex, reaching down to scratch Sally behind the ears. 'I don't know what happened there. Megan's a good dog, and Crooksmoor is normally better than that.'

'Mummy,' said Charlie, pulling on her top. 'I make the doggy do tricks in the field.'

'Shhh,' I said, giving him a nudge.

'No I not shush!' said Charlie. 'I tell Mummy about –'

'Maybe tell me later, Charlie,' said Mum.

Harry the Big smiled. 'Alex, meet my new friends Charlie and Harry.'

Alex ruffled Charlie's hair and smiled at me. Sally the Wonderdog wagged her tail and leaned against my side. 'Good to meet you, kids. I'm a big fan of your Dad's trousers.'

Dad grinned.

'Charlie and Harry were watching you from the top of the field,' said Harry the Big. 'Just eating your sweeties, minding your own business, weren't you kids? Just making a few notes on Crooksmoor's performance, maybe.'

'Uh-huh,' I said. Except I forgot that I had my whistle in my mouth, so a little parp-parp tune came out instead.

Alex frowned for a moment. And then a grin, a chuckle, and finally a great guffaw, a proper Father Christmas belly laugh. 'Nice work, kids. Sounds like I owe you one.'

'Hey,' said Mum. 'It looks like they're announcing the winner.'

'Better get back,' said Alex. 'See you later, Dad. Have a good day, folks.'

The judges, who had been huddled together in the middle of the field, were now at the window of the caravan, talking to the woman. Crooksmoor was leaning on the barrier, staring into space with big bulgy eyes and puffed out cheeks. His dog was nowhere to be seen, and I didn't blame her. Fancy being owned by someone as miserable as that.

The woman switched on her microphone. 'Ladies and Gentlemen, the judges have had a very tricky decision to make, but it gives me great pleasure to announce the winners of this year's Sheep Trial.' She didn't sound like it was giving her great pleasure; in fact she sounded a bit nervous, like she was talking to the headmaster.

'So in third place… ' The woman glanced up from her piece of paper. 'In third place, it's… Sean and Megan!'

As the crowd clapped without much enthusiasm, Crooksmoor ripped off his hat, threw it to the ground and stomped on it with his silly shoes.

'Look!' said Charlie, pointing. 'He naughty again!'

'And in second place, with an almost flawless performance... it's Alex and Sally!'

We cheered. Alex climbed up on the barrier and waved his cap. I caught his eye across the crowd, and I'm sure he winked at me.

A skinny man we didn't know won the sheep competition, so we said goodbye to Harry the Big and left, especially because Charlie was still moaning.

'But you promise!' he kept saying. 'You promise!'

'How about a ride on Daddy's shoulders?' suggested Mum.

'Don't want it.'

'My shoulders?'

'Don't want it.'

'Well there's nothing else to ride, so – oh, look,

Charlie, tractors!'

Mum stopped, and pulled us towards a side field where a sign said 'Ploughing Competition'.

'Seriously?' said Dad. 'A competition to see who can drive a tractor up and down a field to dig the straightest lines? Are you sure there isn't anything more ridiculous we could watch?'

'I'm not sure you're in any position to talk about ridiculous, wearing those trousers,' said Mum. 'I'm surprised they're not queuing up just to look at you. Come on, let's see what's going on.'

This field was right at the edge of the fair. A small viewing platform had been built against a barn wall, so we climbed up. It was packed so we had to jostle to the front, but from there we could see right across the field. Dad was right: farmers were ploughing up and down a field in their tractors. I'm surprised they hadn't crashed it was so boring. More men with clipboards were walking up and down the ends of the rows of soil, kneeling down to look, like it was interesting. Which it wasn't.

As we watched, Crooksmoor turned up and jumped into the nearest tractor. With a wave to the crowd which wasn't returned, he revved the engine and started ploughing a new furrow directly in front of the platform, alongside the hedge.

'I ride a tractor?' asked Charlie, but you could tell by his voice that he didn't think the answer would be yes. Which it wasn't.

'Great trousers!'

A woman a bit younger than Mum, and a bit thinner, and a bit more suntanned, was talking to Dad. She'd pushed her sunglasses up on her head, which was turned on one side to get a better look at Dad's sequinned legs. I'm not surprised she liked them, because hers were leather with diamond studs down the side.

'Err, thanks,' said Dad. You could tell that he didn't know if she was serious. Mum made a face before turning away and pretended to be interested in the ploughing.

'His old ones split, and he's got pink pants on so he didn't want everyone to see them,' I added.

The woman's eyebrows were painted onto her face like two little humpback bridges, but she used some hidden muscles to make them even more pointy.

'Yeah thanks, Harry, I'm not sure this lady's interested in the detail.'

'No seriously, I love them,' she said. 'You can tell a lot about a man from his choice of trousers.'

Mum coughed loudly.

Dad tilted his thigh so the sequins sparkled in the sunshine. 'They do look good, don't they. They remind me of my days in disco.' Dad had to talk louder to be heard above the sound of a nearby tractor engine starting up. 'I used to have some awesome moves on the dance floor. Still got them, as a matter of fact.'

'I can imagine,' said the woman, flashing a smile.

Mum coughed again. It sounded like she was choking on something.

'I like to get these out every now and again, remind me of the good times,' said Dad, stroking his thigh and winking at me.

Mum turned back. 'Tom, did you remember to buy some more nit shampoo? Oh, sorry, I didn't see your new friend. Hello, I'm Tom's *wife*.'

The woman smiled faintly and muttered 'Hi,' before turning back to her friends.

'Who's got nits?' I asked.

'No-one,' said Mum. She chewed her lip as she smiled, and looked at Dad. 'What? Am I cramping your style, Disco Dan?'

'You're just jealous,' said Dad, shaking a hip. 'If you were –'

He was interrupted by a shout we all recognised. 'Mummy! Daddy! I in a tractor!'

Emerging from the barn behind us was a ancient, rusty blue tractor with a plume of blue-black smoke rising from the exhaust. Unlike the other tractors, with their fancy closed cabs and big comfy seats, this one was completely open, with one long bench seat. At the wheel was Alex, and next to him sat Charlie.

Harry the Big was holding the barn door open. 'OK if we take him for a spin?' he shouted up to Mum.

Mum looked at Dad, who shrugged. Mum gave Alex a nervous thumbs up.

And off they went, round the corner of the hedge and up the side of the next field. They didn't have a plough behind them, and this old tractor was pretty nippy. They whizzed up to drive alongside Crooksmoor, and Alex gave him a wave over the hedge. He didn't wave back.

'Do you think Charlie will fall out?' I asked.

'Alex knows what he's doing,' said Harry the

Big, who had joined us on the platform. 'He's been driving that thing since he was your age, maybe younger.'

'What, Charlie's age?' I said.

'I'm not sure I'd put Charlie in charge of a hulking great tractor,' said Dad, smoothing down his sequins.

'Alex would,' I said.

'What?' said Mum and Dad at exactly the same moment.

'Look.'

On the journey back down the field Alex and Charlie had stopped, and Charlie was climbing onto Alex's lap.

'No, Tom, he can't do that!' Mum sounded worried.

'He'll be fine, love,' said Harry the Big. 'Alex won't let him do anything I wouldn't.'

You could see that Charlie had his listening face on as Alex showed him the controls, though how he was supposed to reach them with his chubby little arms and legs I don't know.

The tractor juddered forward, and stopped. Alex took off his red cap, and placed it on Charlie's head, and they were off again.

You could hear Charlie's shrieks of joy from our platform. I was very, very jealous, but I pretended not to be. And it got worse: I thought they'd be driving straight back to the barn and stopping. But slowly the tractor started to turn, before doing a massive loop around the field.

'He's ruining that crop,' said Dad, and sure enough, the tractor was leaving a trail through the green field.

'Not to worry,' said Harry the Big. 'It'll grow back. And if it doesn't, I'll grow it again next year. I'm not worried.'

Dad looked at Harry. 'Is that… your field?'

'Of course it is,' he said. 'They're all my fields. Everything you can see. I can do what I like.'

'Ah,' said Dad, 'that explains a few things.' Not to me, it didn't.

'Where's he going now?' asked Mum.

The tractor was now heading straight for the hedge. Alex had one hand around Charlie, on the wheel, and with the other he was pointing towards a small gap.

'Oh dear,' said Harry, shaking his head. 'This'll put a cat among the pigeons.'

'I can't watch,' said Mum, although I could tell

she was watching through her fingers.

As Charlie and Alex approached the gap, Alex took his hand off the wheel and held his arms in the air.

Charlie had his head down now, staring like crazy at the gap. And do you know, Charlie drove straight through it, without bashing the sides once.

Now on the other side of the hedge, the ploughing competition was still going on, with farmers concentrating hard on their boring straight lines. What they didn't expect was a three-year-old on a tractor, driving all over them and mucking them up.

Several of them did little wobbles all on their own, as soon as they saw Charlie appear through the gap; Alex had crouched down now so you couldn't see him, and it looked like Charlie was driving it on his own.

In fact Charlie was getting the hang of it, and started driving round and round in small circles; at one point I thought he was writing his name with the tyres, but then I remembered he couldn't write.

The crowd had realised what was going on and were laughing like drains. The judges, on the other hand, were hopping mad. Literally hopping mad, jumping up and down like jack-in-the-boxes, and waving their clipboards at Charlie.

'Alex is going to be in so much trouble,' I said to Harry.

'Doesn't matter,' he replied. 'He's off to Australia. And I'm old enough not to care who I upset. You'll get that old one day, it's quite a relief, I can tell you.'

Charlie, on the other hand, was too young to know who he was upsetting, and one person was going to be particularly angry: Crooksmoor. As the farmer nearest the hedge, it was his furrow that Charlie was mucking up most. Crooksmoor himself had turned at the end of the field, and had now stopped his tractor. He was leaning out of his cab, shouting and screaming at Charlie as he circled round again. We couldn't hear what he was saying, because his engine was still on, but I don't think it was polite.

Near our end, Charlie spotted him. With a tug of the wheel – he might have had a little help from Alex – he finished his circle, and started driving towards Crooksmoor. I'd say he was driving straight towards him, but it wasn't straight at all:

Charlie jiggled the steering wheel and the tractor did lots of little wiggles, completely ruining Crooksmoor's furrow.

Crooksmoor himself continued to shout, but you could see he was starting to get worried as Charlie got closer. We were all starting to worry, especially Mum. Harry the Big put his hand on her arm. 'Don't fret,' he said. 'Alex has got this one covered.'

Closer. Closer. Closer. By now Crooksmoor had slid back into his cab, and fumes were rising from his engine as he revved it furiously. But on and on drove Charlie, without slowing even a teensy bit.

Mum screamed. Dad shouted. I yelled. The crowd gasped. A huge, messy crash was definitely, 100% going to –

But it didn't happen. At the very last minute, Alex pulled the steering wheel around from his hidden position, and swerved around Crooksmoor. But Crooksmoor didn't know that was going to happen, and blasted his tractor out of the way. Only he must have pressed a button a bit too hard because he drove it straight into the hedge. The front wheels rose up onto a tree stump and span uselessly in the air.

Crooksmoor slumped back in his seat with his eyes closed, while Alex took the wheel and steered his tractor steadily back to the barn.

Nobody spoke as Alex pulled to a halt and passed Charlie into Mum's outstretched arms. And then there was the sound of someone clapping: steadily and confidently. It was Harry the Big, standing by his barn door.

I looked at him, and at Charlie who was absolutely fine, of course.

I ran down from the platform and stood besides Harry, and clapped along: the two of us, clapping.

Dad left Mum and Charlie, smiled, and joined the clapping gang. The woman on the platform in the sunglasses started clapping. And suddenly everyone was clapping, and cheering, and whooping. Even the farmers in their tractors were clapping.

Everyone, in fact, except Crooksmoor.

I was right, of course: Alex was in a lot of trouble. And because he was with a grown-up, Charlie got away with it, as usual. As we left Alex was talking with the judges, who said he couldn't keep his 2nd place in the Sheep Dog Trial because he'd been so naughty in the ploughing competition. Alex said it was all a stitch-up and that he didn't give a fig, which I thought was a funny thing to give anyway.

'I think we're about done here,' said Mum. 'Time to head for home. Tom!'

Dad was still talking to the sunglasses woman.

'TOM! Come on!'

Dad said something that made the woman laugh like a horse, all teeth and swishy hair, and then joined us.

'Nice to meet you, Harry – do say goodbye to Alex for us,' said Mum.

'Good to meet you too,' said Harry, squeezing my shoulder. 'Don't forget to have a look at the cars on your way out.'

'Look at cars?' said Charlie, sounding confused.

'Old cars. Shiny cars. Cars from the olden days. Mine's the red beauty. Have a sit in it, see what you think. Right, have a safe trip back!'

With a wave, Harry walked off to join Alex; we joined hands and headed for the gate, with Mum and Dad giving Charlie *1-2-3-Wee!* swings between them. They won't do that for me any more because Dad says I'm so heavy I'll pull his arm out of his socket, which I think is just a rubbish excuse.

I cheered up a bit when Dad bought us some candy floss for the walk back. I rolled the pink fluff up into little dark red sugary balls and ate them like sweets. Charlie pushed his whole face into his but that was a bad idea because the stick nearly poked his eye out and he started crying.

We soon saw what Harry the Big had been talking about: in the last field before the exit to the car park a line of old cars glinted in the sun. A few men were shielding their eyes from the glare and peering in the windows.

'Let's not bother,' said Mum. 'I'm exhausted.'

'Look!' said Charlie through his tears. 'Is Harry car!' He was pointing to the only red car, about half way along the row. 'We sit in Harry's car!'

'Do we have to?' I asked. Sitting in cars isn't in my Top 10 hobbies.

Mum sighed. 'Just a quick sit, then we're off.'

Harry's car was quite cool, actually. It had a huge bonnet with slots in the front to make it look mean. It had shiny silver edges to make it look like a party car, and four round headlights to give it funny eyes. And at the front it had two radiators that Dad said were to keep it cool, although I think he meant warm.

Dad sucked in his breath as Charlie rubbed his finger down the side, and pulled him away. 'Probably not a good idea,' he said. 'A shine like that doesn't come easily.'

'I sit in it now?'

Mum looked around. 'Come on then. Just because Harry said so.'

She opened the front door. The inside was as red as the outside: red carpets, red seats, a red dashboard, and a red steering wheel.

'Cool,' I said, and ran round the other side.

'I'm just going to have a squizz at the others while you play,' said Dad to Mum.

'Don't be long, eh?' said Mum. 'Not sure how much longer I can stand.'

For the next ten minutes Charlie sat behind the wheel and pretended to drive me to pre-school. 'Beeb beeb!' he shouted, pressing the horn. 'I drive fast!'

He certainly was driving fast and not carefully either, because he told me he'd knocked down eleventy walls, three hellyfants and a fishfinger.

After he'd pressed every switch he could find and twiddled every dial, he tried to do the windows to talk to Mum, who was outside on her phone. The windows were wind-up though, not electric, and he wasn't strong enough to do that so I leaned across to help him.

'Urgh, Charlie, you've made it all sticky! Mum, Charlie's made the car all sticky!'

'What?' said Mum, looking up. She reached through the window and put her hand on the dashboard. 'Oh Charlie, it's *everywhere!*'

She was right. I hadn't really noticed, but Charlie had left his sticky fingerprints on every surface. The shiny stuff wasn't shiny any more.

'We really need the wipes,' muttered Mum, opening the door and trying to rub the dashboard with her sleeve. 'Where's that disco-loving father of yours when you need him?'

As if he'd heard, Dad strolled up. 'Hi kids! What do you think? I tell you what, there's an amazing car a bit further up, just like the one that James Bond drives.'

'Does it have rockets and everything?' I asked.

'It belongs to that Crooksmoor chap apparently, so I wouldn't be surprised. He's probably had it fitted with lasers to kill kittens. It's gorgeous on the inside, too, all cream seats and beautiful wood – far too nice for that man. I had a cheeky sit in the driver's seat, but then some ape in a suit told me to get out.'

'Tom!' scolded Mum, pulling the wipes from the change bag, and yanking Charlie out of the driver's seat.

'What are you up to, anyway?'

Dad said that to Mum's bottom, which was now sticking out of the car.

'I am cleaning up Charlie's mess, before Harry comes back and wonders why his car feels like… well, feels like ours.'

'Charlie made it all sticky,' I explained.

'Not a good idea,' said Dad. 'People can get a bit twitchy when you mess with their old cars.'

'Like when someone puts your gravy in the wrong place,' I said.

'Exactly,' said Dad, grabbing a wipe. 'Ah, looks like you've finished. Well done.'

Mum stood up, shaking her head.

'Right, time for home, definitely. No more monkeying around. Let's go.'

'Hey, that's the man from the tractor!' I'd

recognise that angry man anywhere now, and he was stomping towards us. He had his head down, and hadn't spotted us.

'Tom, take Charlie,' said Mum quietly.

'Good idea. I'm not sure you're his favourite three-year-old right now,' said Dad, scooping Charlie into his arms. 'Keep over, let's stay out of his way.'

Crooksmoor marched right past us without noticing and we all breathed out. I don't think any of us had even realised we'd been holding our breath.

'Well that was a good day, in the end,' said Mum. 'Now how do we get back to the car?'

'Across there.' I pointed. 'Look, we can take a short-cut across the field to that gate.'

Charlie was now riding high on top of Dad's shoulders. 'Could you stop pulling my hair, Charlie?'

'I looking for nits,' he said, pulling out a strand of Dad's hair and holding it up.

'Ow! I'm pretty sure I'm nit-free,' said Dad, 'and soon I'll be hair free.'

'Found one! I the Nit Hunter,' said Charlie.

'What?' I said.

'Only joking,' said Charlie, grinning.

'I didn't know he did jokes,' said Mum. 'Maybe he has found one. Anyway, Charlie, what was your favourite bit of the day?'

'Daddy's pinky pants.'

'That was mine too,' said Mum.

'And me,' I added.

'Funnily enough, that wasn't mine,' said Dad. 'I'll be glad to get these trousers off too, they're rubbing in places that trousers shouldn't.' Dad did a little jiggle to see if he could make himself more comfy.

'I'd half forgotten you were wearing them,' said Mum, but she was interrupted by the sound of a man shouting, very very loudly.

We looked round. 'It's Crooksmoor,' I said. He was standing next to a light blue sports car. He was bellowing at a big man dressed in a dark suit that didn't fit him, like a sausage bursting out of its skin, and certainly looked a bit silly in the middle of a field. Crooksmoor kept waving at the car, and then yanked open the door and pointed inside.

'I wonder what the matter is,' I said.

'Tom?' Mum said. 'Is that the guy in the suit

the one who told you to get out? You didn't do anything daft, did you?'

'No, of course not!' replied Dad, but I could see he was looking a little unsure. 'Shh! What's he saying?'

We all tried to hear Crooksmoor (except Charlie who was looking for nits in Dad's hair). It wasn't hard, his voice boomed across the field.

'PURPLE! PURPLE! THERE'S BLOOMIN PURPLE ALL OVER MY BLOOMIN SEATS!'

Mum and Dad looked at each other. And then Mum looked down at Dad's trousers.

'Do you think...?'

Dad looked down, and rubbed his hand on the bum of his sequinned bellbottoms. He turned it palm outwards: it was a pale, but unmistakable shade of purple. Unlike Dad's face, which went quite white.

'HIM! THERE!'

'Dad,' I said. 'Dad. DAD. DAD!' I pointed.

The sausage-shaped man was also pointing, but unfortunately he was pointing at us. Crooksmoor wasn't pointing, but that wasn't a good thing because he was running. Towards us. Like a raging bull.

'Uh-oh,' said Dad. 'Not sure I like the look of this. Quick – RUN!'

I screamed and grabbed Mum's hand. We turned and sprinted for the gate. Charlie wobbled all over the place on Dad's shoulders, which he loved of course. 'He coming, Daddy! He very fast!'

I didn't dare look back. The gate into the car park field was half open. Dad and Charlie ran through first, then me, then Mum.

'Close it!' shouted Dad.

Mum yanked me to a stop as she turned and heaved the heavy gate closed. We both yelped as we saw Crooksmoor who was now half way across the field.

'STOP THE HIPPY!' he was shouting as he ran. 'STOP. THE. HIPPY!'

Our car wasn't far. Dad fished the keys out of the change bag as he ran and bibbed the button, holding it for too long so all the windows went down as well.

'Are you a hippy Daddy?' shouted Charlie, still enjoying the ride. 'Can I be a hippy? What's a hippy?'

'Never mind that,' he said, swinging Charlie down. 'Liz, get the kids in, I'll start the engine!'

and he jumped into the driver's seat.

'Quick, Mum!' I shouted, scrambling into my seat and fumbling with my seatbelt.

'I Am Being Quick!' humphed Mum as she tried to buckle Charlie in. 'I want pick up my narna skin,' he said, trying to get out again, but Mum was too strong and pushed him back into his seat. Click! Done.

I looked back to the gate. Crooksmoor must have had trouble opening it, because now he was climbing over, his silly tartan legs waving everywhere, trying to find a foothold as he rolled his belly over the top.

Dad had started the engine. 'Quick! For goodness sake Liz, get in!'

Mum slammed Charlie's door and ran round the back. Dad started driving forwards towards the exit gate. Meanwhile Crooksmoor had picked himself up off the floor, and was now just a few metres away, close enough for us to see his bright red sweaty face and hear his angry grunts.

'Mum!' I yelled.

Mum was jogging alongside the car, trying to open the passenger door. But the field was really bumpy, and she couldn't get a grip on the handle.

'Tom, slow down!'

'I can't!' Dad shouted back. 'He'll throttle me! We're nearly there, you've got to get in!'

'Tom, you've got to stop, I don't think I can make it!' Mum couldn't keep up.

'Dad! Slow down! We can't leave Mum behind!'

Mum had fallen back and was now alongside my door, but we were nearly at the exit – a narrow gate onto the road. The door would be snapped straight off if she opened it now.

Mum grabbed the edges of my open window. 'Aaaaarrrrgh!' she yelled and with a big jump, pushed her top half straight through my window, landing on my lap.

'Gnurff shnugg!' she shouted, or something like that: it was hard to tell because she had her face squashed into my legs. I took hold of her trousers and pulled as hard as I can, and with a couple of wriggles she plopped through, onto the seat. Charlie looked at her, and for once he was open-mouthed: he couldn't believe his eyes.

'GO GO GO!' shouted Mum. We reached the road and if Dad needed any more encouragement to go like the wind he got it, because Crooksmoor had caught us up now and was banging on the rear windscreen, screaming and yelling about bad hippies.

With a screech of tyres and the beep of a horn from a car coming down the road, Dad accelerated away. I finally dared to look back; Crooksmoor was stood in the middle of the road, his waistcoat ripped and his shirt hanging out, shaking his fist at us like someone in a cartoon.

Around the next bend, Dad pulled into a lay-by. Everyone was silent for a moment, except for Mum who grunted a bit more as she climbed into her seat.

'You OK?' said Dad, looking at her.

Mum looked back. 'I might be,' she said. She had an angry mouth, but smiley eyes. 'No thanks to you and your silly hippy games.'

'What's a hippy?' asked Charlie again.

'It's someone who's old, and wears silly clothes, and sometimes is smelly,' I said. 'We did it at school.'

'Ah,' said Charlie. 'Like Daddy.'

'That's right,' said Mum.

'And Mummy.'

'That's not right,' said Mum.

'You did great, by the way,' said Dad. 'Back there. Your move with the car window.'

'Yeah Mum, you were amazing,' I said.

'Like a wiggly worm,' said Charlie.

'Thanks,' said Mum. 'I was pretty great, wasn't I.' She grinned.

I was trapped in car with a smelly hippy, a wiggly worm and the Nit Hunter. Just another family day out.

Read on...for free!

If you enjoyed this third collection of stories about Harry and Charlie, I have another story waiting for you – completely free!

I occasionally send out emails to tell readers and their parents about new Charlie stories, other books that are in the pipeline, and stuff I think you'll enjoy.

Get your Mum or Dad to sign up for my emails and I'll whizz over the Festival eBook – an eye-popping Charlie adventure featuring a fortune teller, crunchy pastries and a very hairy man from Australia. It's packed with fun and it'll do enough bedtimes to last until the weekend. After that, I'm afraid you're on your own.

Sound good? Ask someone big to sign up for my emails now at **matwaugh.co.uk/freeminibook**

One last thing...

Did these stories make you laugh? Did chocolate milk shake spurt out of your nose, and perhaps all over your Mum, Dad or dog? Did you start coughing on your own dribble until your Mum, Dad or dog had to slap you on the back?

If so, please do me one big favour. Get a grown-up to sign in so you can write a review on Amazon. Don't hang about. Do it today. You can even make up a name so nobody will know it's you. You'll immediately feel a warm glow spreading from your fingertips, and you will *definitely* get extra pudding.

If, on the other hand, you only got this far because you're pressing dried flowers between each page, then why not try one of my other books? You might like it and we could still be friends!

Also by Mat Waugh

Cheeky Charlie
From Amazon. Free eBook: matwaugh.co.uk

Cheeky Charlie: Bugs and Bananas (Book 2)
Available now from Amazon.

Cheeky Charlie: He Didn't Mean It (Book 4)
Available soon!

Cheeky Charlie: Festival
Free for subscribers. **matwaugh.co.uk/freebook**

Coming soon for older children:

The Fun Factor
In a remote village, the stuff everyone loves is disappearing by the day. First to go is the internet. Next up: phones, pizzas, TV channels and even the dishwasher. Twelve-year-old Thora and her friends struggle to see what's so fun about the good old days, but soon discover they're guinea pigs in a decidedly high-tech social experiment...

About Mat Waugh

I'm a father of three young girls. I'm often tired. These two things are connected.

I live in Tunbridge Wells, which is a lively, lovely town in the south east of England.

Small boys scare me – they do too much running, and not enough drawing. But I'm petrified by the thought of three teenage girls.

When I was seven I wrote to Clive King. He's the author of my favourite childhood book, *Stig of the Dump*, which is about a caveman who lives in a house made out of rubbish. I asked Clive if there was going to be a sequel, but he said no.

I've had lots of writing and editing jobs, but mostly for other people.

I forgot: I also had a crazy year when I thought I wanted to be a teacher. But then I found out how hard teachers work, and that you have to buy your own biscuits. So I stopped, and now I just visit schools to eat theirs and talk to children about stories.

That letter from Clive King gave me the idea that I could write my own stories, but I could never find the right moment. So I waited until I had children and had no spare time at all. If you want something done, ask a busy person.

I started writing about Charlie because I want to make children laugh, without making the grown-ups sigh, or cry. Grown-ups will know what I mean.

I'm also writing books for slightly older children. The stories are a bit more scary, and there aren't as many bottom jokes.

One more thing: I love hearing from readers. Funny stuff, silly stuff, serious stuff. Any kind of stuff, in fact. If that's you, then please get in touch.

✉ mail@matwaugh.co.uk
www.matwaugh.co.uk

Or, if you're old enough:

❦ facebook.com/matwaughauthor
❦ twitter.com/matwaugh

31006665R00079

Printed in Great Britain
by Amazon